THE SKELTON GIRL

1812: These are tempestuous times in the wool mills of the Pennine moors. Randolf Staines is introducing new machinery to Keld Mill, which will put many of the villagers out of work. Diana Skelton, whose father used to own Keld Mill, takes a strong dislike to Randolf, and when there is trouble amongst the dismissed croppers she becomes involved. It is only after a night of violence at the mill that Diana and Randolf begin to see eye to eye . . .

GILLIAN KAYE

THE SKELTON GIRL

Complete and Unabridged

LINFORD
Leicester

First published in Great Britain in 2007

First Linford Edition
published 2007

British Library CIP Data

Kaye, Gillian
    The Skelton girl.—Large print ed.—
Linford romance library
    1. Strikes and lockouts—Textile industry
—England, Northern—History—19th
century—Fiction 2. England, Northern
—Social conditions—19th century—Fiction
3. Love stories 4. Large type books
I. Title
823.9'2 [F]

ISBN 978–1–84617–988–4

Published by
F. A. Thorpe (Publishing)
Anstey, Leicestershire

Set by Words & Graphics Ltd.
Anstey, Leicestershire
Printed and bound in Great Britain by
T. J. International Ltd., Padstow, Cornwall

This book is printed on acid-free paper

1

When Diana came back into Keld Head House after her ride on the moor, she took off her shoes and went into the drawing-room expecting to find Corinne there. She stopped inside the door with a start of surprise for instead of the pretty eighteen-year-old who was her sister, she was confronted by her father and a tall, striking-looking gentleman who was a complete stranger to her.

'Diana, my dear, you have come back at last. I wished you to meet Mr Randolf Staines who is to be the new owner of Keld Mill. Mr Staines, this is my daughter, Diana.

She found herself staring as the gentleman made his bow to her. For this was a young man and obviously a gentleman from the cut of his coat and the set of his cravat; very tall, dark hair worn rather short, and startlingly blue eyes in a face which could only be described as handsome.

This was no usual owner of any cloth mill. She had been prepared to dislike the man who was to take her father's place at the mill.

But she gave him her hand. 'I am pleased to welcome you to Holmby,' she said civilly enough.

Her father spoke before the stranger could make any reply. 'I think I will leave you to become acquainted with Mr Staines while I go and draw up the contract which we are to sign when Mr Barraclough, the lawyer, comes tomorrow morning. I had hoped that Corinne would be here, but I expect she has gone off to the Rectory to see the Gilchrist boys.'

Mr Josiah Skelton left the room and his eldest daughter found herself standing uncomfortably in front of the stranger. Her father was the owner of three woollen mills in a moorland area to the south of Huddersfield in the West

Riding of Yorkshire. Hawkshead and Firth mills were both small and had been in the valley for hundreds of years, but Keld Mill had been built by her grandfather in the late 1770s. Until this time, Mr Skelton had managed the bigger mill himself; but recently he had to decide to sell it.

'Keld seems to be a common name around here, Miss Skelton.'

Diana replied readily. 'Yes, it is the River Keld which flows past the mill; our house and the mill take the same name. Do you know the area?'

He shook his head. 'No, I am from Swaledale in the north of the country, more accustomed to lead mines than woollen mills.'

Diana could feel an awkwardness in the conversation and wished her father had not left her on her own with the stranger. She found herself thinking that if they walked outside, perhaps it would be easier for her to say what she wanted to make clear to the new owner of Keld Mill.

She was a young lady of four-and-twenty, rather tall and angular; however, what she lacked in grace, she gained in beauty. Her hair was a deep, rich auburn, her eyes dark and her skin pale. Her family and friends thought of her as beautiful, but Diana knew herself to be awkward.

'Mr Staines,' she said as pleasantly as she could. 'I would be pleased to show you the view from Keld Head House, it will give you some idea of the area. Would you like to walk in the grounds with me?'

His reply was swift. 'Certainly, Miss Skelton, I would welcome it.'

She looked at him, suddenly doubting his sincerity, but she walked towards the door which he held open for her.

Keld Head House had been built over two hundred years before by a previous owner of the Keld mills; it was situated above the valley and had a commanding position. Behind it rose the wild moorland which Diana loved so much and below lay the village of Holmby which was dominated by the Keld Mill.

The garden of Keld Head House was terraced and being the early spring of 1812, the terraces were bright with daffodils and crocuses which had been planted between the trees and shrubs by previous Skeltons.

'This is a splendid position for a house,' said their visitor, looking around him. 'But don't you find it cold up here, Miss Skelton?'

She smiled. 'Yes, we do catch the winds, but it is always fresh and I suppose I find it invigorating.'

'You like the outdoors?' he asked her.

He really is quite civil, Diana thought, I must forget that I was prepared to dislike him. 'Yes, I am very fond of riding, and the moor is always tempting even in the winter.'

She turned and looked past the house towards the high moorland. 'You can see that the moor is inviting. Look closely and you can see both our smaller mills, they are very old and powered by water. My father has put steam into Keld Mill, I expect he has shown you; he thinks that a younger man would do better at Keld Mill.'

She paused as they negotiated the steep steps between the terraces, his hand at her elbow. 'You have experience of the woollen industry, Mr Staines?'

'A little,' he replied shortly. 'I have recently spent a year in the worsted mills of Bradford.'

'That is more than a little, as you put it. The Bradford mills are considered the finest in the area. I am surprised you are tempted into such a small concern as Keld Mill.'

He gave a surprising grin. 'There is a world of difference between being a weaver in Bradford and becoming the owner of Keld Mill.'

'You cannot be serious,' she exclaimed. 'I could never believe that you worked as a weaver, it is obvious that you are a gentleman.'

'Reckon you'll find me out, lass,' he replied in the dialect of one of the Bradford weavers he had been working amongst.

Diana was finding it difficult to come to terms with the personality of Mr Randolf Staines. She had certainly met no one quite like him before and there were going to be some awkward questions to ask. Dare she approach him on this their first meeting?

'I think you like to be enigmatic, Mr Staines, I am used to dealing with plain-spoken local men and getting straight answers.'

He did not reply immediately; he was looking down the valley and at the mill in particular.

'Do you mean you have dealings with the mill, ma'am? Do your parents not keep you sheltered from the troubles that you must have there?'

Diana hesitated. 'I think my father cannot have told you that he is a widower; my mother died two years ago and I run the house for him.'

'I am sorry, I had no idea,' was all he said in reply.

'Thank you, sir,' Diana was surprised at his courtesy and hesitated before asking the question she was burning to ask him.

'I would like to ask your intentions when you take over the mill.'

'My intentions?' he asked crisply.

'Yes, there is talk of bringing in cropping frames and I am very concerned.'

'You are concerned, ma'am?'

'Is there any reason why I should not be concerned?' She asked the question with some irritation. 'I have grown up amongst the families who work in the mill, you must understand that. If you worked in Bradford, you probably know of the trouble we are having with the breaking up of the machinery in the mills. That same trouble seems to be creeping nearer to us, Mr Staines.'

He nodded, but said nothing and Diana continued.

'You will know what the main

problem is with the introduction of cropping frames. Men who raise the nap on the cloth, then crop it smooth with shears are being put out of work; I have heard that one cropping frame does the work of ten men and it needs only one man to operate it. It does not take much arithmetic to work out that nine men are put out of work for each frame installed; they suffer for there is no work elsewhere, and their wives and children suffer, too.'

'You know a lot about these things, Miss Skelton,' he observed dryly.

'Of course I do,' she snapped. 'I am opposed to such violence, but I am also opposed to the men having no work and their families suffering because new machinery is being brought in.'

'But, Miss Skelton, your father and his forbears must have brought in new machines when they built Keld Mill.'

'I am not a simpleton, Mr Staines. It is almost one hundred years ago since the men wove the cloth in their cottages and their wives did the spinning, the new machines meant more production and work for all. The arrival of the cropping frames is a different matter.'

Randolf Staines was watching her closely. Here was a surprising young lady, he was thinking. Almost a beauty with that lovely red hair, and not afraid to say what she thought. Perhaps Keld Mill at Holmby won't be such a quiet little backwater after all, he told himself.

'I trust that you will not stir up the local mill workers against me, Miss Skelton, I am quite determined on the frames, you know.' He spoke quite seriously.

'If I have anything at all to do with it,' she replied crisply, 'it will be to organise the distribution of food for all the stricken families. It should be possible, at the least, to get together bags of oats so that the children can be given their porridge. And I believe we could make a collection so that the men who have lost their work can go over to Barnsley and bring back some coal.'

'What does your father think of the cropping frames?' he asked her and saw a sad expression pass over her face.

'Poor Papa, he has aged since Mama died and wishes to avoid the problems with the introduction of new methods though he does realise that they must come in time. I think that is why he has sold the mill to you.' She looked at him keenly. 'Will you bring in the frames, Mr Staines?'

'It is my intention, yes. We always look for improvements in the ways of producing cloth. Will you oppose me, ma'am?' he asked and she thought his tone disapproving.

'You will find me on the side of those with no work and no food to give their children.' Diana replied frostily. 'I certainly do not call putting men out of work an improvement as you put it.' She could feel herself losing patience.

'But have you not thought, that if we can produce more cloth then we will sell more? Our mills can increase production and that in itself will bring more work for the men.'

Diana tossed her head scornfully. She was still wearing her russet-coloured riding dress and looked magnificent. 'You are trying to pacify me, sir. It is foolish of you, for you must know that I am aware of the Orders in Council which prohibit you from selling your cloth on the continent. As long as the war with France goes on, you have lost your foreign markets.'

By this time, they had reached the lower part of the garden and were standing under a splendid beech tree which was beginning to show the tender green of the first leaves of the year.

They had paused and were facing each other; an onlooker would have called it a confrontation. Randolf Staines put out a hand and gripped her arm fiercely.

'You do not lack for answers, Miss Skelton; I think I will look forward to my visits to Keld Head House. But first, I want to be assured that I do not have any opposition from you when the cropping frames arrive.'

Diana stayed very still. She could feel the hurt of his fingers through the cloth of her coat, but made no sign. Here was a gentleman to be reckoned with and she did not want any open clash with him on the day of his arrival.

'I can assure you, sir,' she said and thought that she sounded haughty, 'that my first concern will be with the women and children of Holmby. I feel certain that you have already made plans to protect your frames.'

He released his hold on her arm. 'It is so, Miss Skelton, shall we return to the house?'

No more was said between them, but Diana had the sudden notion that she was going to dislike this gentleman. His intention of installing cropping frames in Keld Mill would have given her good enough reason, but now she was faced with a sharp, sardonic tongue. She changed the subject abruptly.

'I think my sister, Corinne, will have

returned, sir, please come up to the house and meet her.'

Corinne Skelton was indeed in the drawing-room, having returned to Keld Head House while Diana was in the garden with Mr Staines, she had not liked to go after them and was waiting impatiently indoors for them to return.

She was a small girl, not just lacking in height, but delicately boned. She had fair hair and an appealing face with small mouth and large blue eyes. She was regarded as a very pretty girl indeed. A greater contrast to her older sister it would have been impossible to find. Anyone who had been acquainted with Mrs Skelton would have known that while Corinne took after her mother, Diana favoured her father.

Diana went to her and took her by the hand. 'I am pleased that you are at home, Corinne, I wish you to meet the new owner of Keld Mill. Mr Staines, this is my sister, Corinne.'

Then she watched as Randolf Staines made a very formal bow. She saw an expression come into Corinne's face which showed an instant adoration in the girl's eyes.

Oh dear, thought Diana, surely Corinne is not going to fall in love with Mr Staines, he is much too old for her. She listened to their exchange of words.

'I am charmed, Miss Skelton,' said the gentleman politely.

Corinne flushed and there was an excitement in her voice. 'Oh, please call me Corinne. Miss Skelton sounds so formal and that is Diana in any case.'

'Certainly, Corinne, it will please me for it is a very pretty name, and for a very pretty girl, if I might say so.'

Diana glared at him. He is turning on the charm, damn him, she muttered to herself.

'You said something, Miss Skelton?' he asked, looking away from Corinne.

'No, I did not,' Diana replied ungraciously. 'I may have something to say later on.'

'Certainly, ma'am.' He turned back to Corinne. 'Do you ride, Corinne?

Perhaps you would care to come riding with me and show me some of the best places for a good gallop.'

Corinne shook her head, a rueful expression on her face. 'I never ride. I was thrown from my pony when I was small and have disliked horses ever since. I still have a pony, but I do not go far. It is Diana you must ask, she rides everywhere, even down to the village if she is visiting.'

'Never mind,' he replied. 'Perhaps we can walk in the garden when I am free, thought I am afraid that will not be very often. And, Corinne, please call me Randolf, I do not like to be formal.'

'Yes, of course, Randolf, if you wish,' breathed Corinne and Diana could see that her sister was bewitched. He encouraged her, she fumed. Randolf indeed.

She fought her annoyance as her father came into the room. 'Ah, Staines, there you are and you have met Corinne, I see. I am pleased about that, but do watch her, for she's a naughty little puss and I am afraid that she would carry on a flirtation at a single word of encouragement from you. I spoil her, I must confess, since losing my wife a few years ago.

'No doubt, Diana will have told you of my misfortune, but Diana is a good girl and runs the house for me as well as any housekeeper. She is very capable and willing. Now, I wish to show you the contract which has been drawn up. Please come into the library.'

Diana was left chuckling over the rapt expression on Corinne's face. 'Well, what do you think of the new mill owner, little sister?' she asked playfully.

'I have never met such a fine or handsome gentleman, Diana. Frederick Gilchrist at the Rectory has always been my hero until now, but as he is up at Oxford; I see very little of him. He is always very pleasant and he is so studious, I expect he will go into the church like his father.'

Diana frowned. 'Corinne, it does not say much for your judgement if you are belittling a young gentleman because his intention is to enter the priesthood.'

Corinne was not put out by the rebuke. 'I admire Frederick very much and he has always said that he would marry me one day, but he is very dull. Randolf — don't you think that it is a romantic name? He is so handsome and so very much the gentleman even if he is to be the mill owner.'

Her sister sighed and gave up; nothing would ever change the frivolous nature of the pretty girl. She loved Corinne dearly, but could wish for a little more common sense in her make up. Now there was the arrival on the scene of Randolf Staines. Diana could foresee problems ahead in more ways than one.

That afternoon, Mr Skelton took his guest down to Keld Mill. The next morning the lawyer, Mr Barraclough, arrived at Keld Head House and the papers were signed. Keld Mill had a new owner. Another visit to the mill was made and that evening, Mr

Randolf Staines stayed to have dinner with them.

He took little notice of either Diana or Corinne, and Diana could see that her young sister looked quite put out. She had dressed for the occasion in her favourite dress of a soft blue sarsenet and did succeed in looking very lovely; but it did not impress their visitor who had much to say to his host on matters concerning the mill.

Once the tea-tray had been brought in, he became more sociable and joked with Corinne until her cheeks were pink with delight. Diana despaired.

As their guest rose to go, he addressed himself to Diana. 'Miss Skelton, might I have the honour of a few words with you on your own? Your father has given me permission to use the library.'

Diana stood up in surprise; she was looking particularly handsome in a plain green dress of Norwich crepe, its only ornament being a trim of chenille around the low neck and the hem. She was a slim girl and the fashionably low bodice of her dress showed the gentle swell of her breasts to an appealing advantage.

Although surprised by their visitor's request, she showed no embarrassment and took his arm as he led her from the room.

In the library, he held out a chair for her in front of the fire, then stood with his back to the fireplace, facing her and looking very serious. He said nothing, and feeling embarrassed, Diana made herself speak first.

'You look very serious, Mr Staines.'

His expression did not change, but he nodded. 'Diana — yes, I am going to call you Diana. I have already insisted on your sister's first name, and as we are sure to become well-acquainted when I move into Mill House, I see no need for any formality. I would ask you to call me Randolf.'

'Certainly, if that is what you wish,' she said rather stiffly.

'Yes, I do wish it. I have a particular

reason for wishing it.'

'Sir?' Diana was mystified and somewhat intrigued.

'Miss Skelton . . . Diana, it is just over twenty-four hours since we first met. In that time, you have impressed me with your sincerity, your forthrightness, and I might also say, with your beauty . . .'

'Sir,' again just the one word, but she wanted to interrupt this strange flow of compliments.

'No, please do not interrupt, I wish to make some explanation. I am thirty-five years of age, I believe you to be four-and-twenty. Until now, I have had no wish to marry; the young ladies I have been acquainted with have lacked any personality or seriousness of purpose. But I had made up my mind that if I was to become the owner of Keld Mill, it was time that I looked for a wife. I had imagined that there would be many families in the area with daughters seeking the married state.

'What I had not imagined was that

on my arrival here, I should immediately meet a young lady who would fulfil the role of my wife to perfection. In other words, Diana, I am asking you if you would do me the honour of becoming my wife.'

It would be an understatement to say that Diana was surprised. She was startled, shocked, taken aback, all of those things; she jumped up to face Randolf Staines.

'Sir, you leave me almost speechless. How can you possibly have decided in the space of twenty-four hours that I would make you a suitable wife? I consider the proposal an insult to myself and a lack of judgement on your part. We would disagree instantly. I will tell you quite open that I have taken you in dislike; we have already differed on the question of the cropping frames. But that is not the main reason for my objection.'

'You have other reasons, ma'am?' he asked with a certain irony.

She glared at him. 'I suppose it would

be only polite of me — I do not lack civility — to thank you for your offer, but I must decline it. I have to decline it. I am already engaged to be married to another gentleman; he is Mr Gilbert Dyke and he owns Cannock Hall which is on the other side of Holmby.'

2

There was a taut silence in the library of Keld Head House. Diana, in her astonishment and confusion, saw a mixture of expressions come into her companion's face; surprise certainly, and she could see regret, even anger?

She had to be honest with herself and admit that since her first meeting with the new mill owner, she had not once thought of Gilbert Dyke.

She had been engaged to be married to Mr Dyke for over a year and their wedding was planned for later in the summer. It was an advantageous match for Diana, but thinking of Gilbert now, she could understand why any thought of him had been eclipsed by the arrival of Mr Randolf Staines.

Diana had known Gilbert all her life. The Dyke family owned Cannock Hall on the other side of Holmby and

Gilbert, the eldest of the Dyke's three boys, had been fond of riding in the direction of Keld Head House.

He and Diana had always been on good terms and when he had asked her hand in marriage, she had accepted despite realising that although she was fond of him, she did not love him as she had expected to love the man she was to marry. She had been three-and-twenty at the time and having met no-one she could come near to loving, she had accepted the dull and proper Gilbert very gladly.

At that time, Gilbert's father had just died and Gilbert had taken up the reins of the large estate at Cannock Hall; he felt that he should mourn his father for a year, and so Diana had entered into a long, but not unpleasant engagement.

Thinking of him now, she could not understand how he could have slipped from her mind for the best part of two days.

But looking up at the almost frowning Randolf Staines, she thought that perhaps it was not surprising that Gilbert had vanished from her thoughts.

'Did you hear me, sir?' she asked him.

'Miss Skelton . . . Diana, there had been no hint of any engagement either from your father or yourself. Is that Mr Gilbert Dyke such an insignificant person?'

Diana jumped up and faced him. 'How dare you. You come here not yet the owner of the mill, you are domineering, you are insulting. Why should I have mentioned anything about Gilbert to you? It is none of your concern. If I have not mentioned him, it is because he is a quiet and gentle person.

'Today I have been forced to think of matters concerning the mill which are neither quiet nor gentle.' She paused and took a breath. 'Not only that, how can you possibly ask marriage of a person you have known only a few hours?'

'I have taken a liking to you, Diana. I

think I would like to kiss you, would you object?'

She glared at him, feeling all the more angry because she felt an inward urge which seemed to tell her that she would like to be kissed by him.

'Of course I would object, you are no gentleman and I will take myself off on my horse rather than have to endure your company. We are going to regret the day you ever came to Keld Mill.'

He gave a mocking bow and turned towards the door.

'I admire you, Miss Skelton, goodnight.'

As the door clicked shut, Diana sat in her chair again. Her senses were reeling; her mind was confused with the impact of this Randolf Staines on her person. Stiff with anger and outrage, she gripped the arms of her chair. Thank goodness I have Gilbert, she told herself, at least he is a gentleman and we are soon to be married. I can forget the mill owner.

But can I, echoed in her brain, as she

said goodnight to her father and went upstairs to her bedroom. Lying in bed, she could not dismiss the gentleman from her memory or her feeling and she had to admit that there was something very forceful about him.

Thank goodness I have Gilbert, she thought, but perversely found that the personality of Gilbert Dyke seemed pale in comparison to that of Randolf Staines. At last, she drifted into sleep, but it came uneasily and she found her dreams haunted by the two men who were uppermost in her mind.

I must talk to Gilbert, she decide on waking, he will be keen to hear about the new owner of Keld Mill. But first, I will call and see Annie Netheroyd in the village, she will want to know what Mr Staines has decided about the cropping frames. She will not be pleased.

She breakfasted before Corinne had appeared and was thankful. She felt herself to be in a serious mood and would not have welcomed Corinne's chatter.

It had always been Diana's custom to visit her father's people in the village. She had always thought of them as her father's people as every man living in Holmby worked in the mill. From being a small child, she had gone with her mother to take provisions for the villagers if a new child was born or if someone was sick.

After her mother's death, she had undertaken the task willingly on her own, riding down from Keld Head House to the village and always making her first call the cottage of Annie Netheroyd.

Annie knew everything that was going on in Holmby and soon directed Diana to the families who needed the most help. Her husband, Zach, as she called him, was a cropper at the mill and as Diana rode quietly down the hill that morning, she could feel a sense of dread at having to tell Annie about the cropping frames.

The track was stony and she always made Chester, her favourite mare, take it very slowly. In front of her lay the large village clustered at the foot of the hill; the main street was no more than two rows of stone houses and cottages of various sizes; each cottage had its *piece* of land at the back where vegetables were grown and hens were kept. The church stood solemnly at the end of the street and slightly up the hill. The graveyard at its side was sadly often used.

At the other end of the village on lower ground by the river, and dominating the landscape stood the mill; behind it and higher up on the moor was Mill House which would become the new owner's property and his home.

Mill House had stood empty for some years, its last occupant being Mr Skelton's brother who had helped him to run the mill. When he had died, his widow and children had moved to Leeds to live and Mr Skelton had put a housekeeper into Mill House. It had remained well-furnished and well-cared for and Diana wondered if the new owner would keep on Mrs Buckden, who was the housekeeper.

These matters were passing through her mind as she rode into the village. All the dwellings were of the local stone, dark and solemn, brightened only by the colours of the curtains at the small windows. Odd lengths of cloth were easily come by in a mill town.

Diana picked her way carefully along the cobbles between the neatly kept cottages and made her way to Annie Netheroyd's. Annie's cottage was smaller than most, but it must have been the neatest and cleanest in the whole village.

Leaving Chester at the door, where she knew the mare would wait patiently, Diana gave a quick knock, but did not wait to be admitted. Annie always insisted that she knocked and walked straight in.

Annie Netheroyd was forty years of age and looked nearer sixty; her face was lined, but the lines of worry did not show as she greeted Diana.

'Miss Diana,' she said straight out with no greeting. 'You've got news of new owner of mill, I were expecting you, lass. Sit on Zach's chair and tell me what's to happen then. Is it frames?'

In the one living-room, there were two chairs at the fireside and a small table where the family ate their meals. The only other piece of furniture was a dresser which held not only cracked cups and mugs, but colourful plates of which Annie was very proud.

Diana looked round at the familiar scene which though bare and plain, was usually a happy place. Two small children, Tom and Mary, were playing with building blocks made by their father, baby Netheroyd was on Annie's lap. The eldest boy, always known as Small Zach and his brother, Georgy, were missing, both of them at the mill with their father.

Diana knew that Annie was waiting for her to speak. 'Annie, I'm sorry to bring bad news, but I suppose we were expecting it,' she began, leaning towards the older woman and speaking quietly so that children would not hear the note of worry in her voice. 'I have met the new owner, his name is Mr Randolf Staines and he is younger than I imagined he would be. He tells me that he is going to bring in the cropping frames.'

'Oh, Miss Diana, what'll us do?' Annie Netheroyd did not sob or cry. She looked at Diana and tears trickled slowly down her cheeks. 'It's hard enough now, but what if Zach is thrown out of work? And I worry about him. He's a good man, no doubt about that, but he's a hot-head and I can't deny it. He won't take this news quietly, that's for sure; I'm afeard for him, afeard he'll get into some sort of trouble.'

The tears did come then. 'What'll us do? What'll we do with no wage coming in? They say as it'll take one man to do the work that ten used to do, that's all them families with their menfolk taking nowt home. And we got to eat, Miss Diana, we got to eat. I knows as we've got a few hens out back and I can give bairns an egg sometimes, but we need milk from farms and oats, too, if I'm to give them their porridge. They don't see much meat except for a scrap of bacon when we can manage it or sometimes a rabbit if Zach's lucky.'

Diana had let Annie have her say, she needed to air her woes. They were many and not the least being afraid of Zach's reaction to his loss of work. She thought quickly and spoke slowly.

'Annie, the frames are not in the mill yet. I will speak with Mr Staines again and see if I can make him change his mind.'

She knew she was giving Annie false hopes, but she stood up and looked at the children, they had stopped their game when they saw that their mother was upset and had gathered round her. Annie put her arm round them, fiercely protective. She tried to smile.

Diana bent down and gave the worn

face a kiss. 'I will help you somehow, Annie, you can trust me.'

Tears came again to Annie's eyes, this time they were of gratitude. 'You is a one, Miss Diana, but I knows I can trust you.'

'I will go now, Annie, and you are not to worry.'

She spoke lightly, but she walked out of the cottage and jumped up on Chester with a heavy heart.

* * *

In the time Diana had been with Annie Netheroyd, her fiancé, Mr Gilbert Dyke of Cannock Hall, had ridden to Keld Head House to see her. He knew that she had been expecting a visit from the new owner of the mill and he was eager for news of this Randolf Staines who was a stranger to him.

Gilbert had been only twenty-eight when his father had died the previous year, and now, at nearly thirty years of age, he managed the large estate of

Cannock Hall with energy and competence. He had four farms scattered over the moor, three of them being sheep farms.

Hope Farm at Cannock Hall was lower down the slope of the moors and the richer soil produced wheat, oats and barely, here too was the dairy herd and the village of Holmby was kept well supplied with milk, butter and cheese.

Gilbert was mild-tempered and hard-working; anyone seeing him riding up the track to Keld Head House would have described him as an ordinary young gentleman. He lacked height and his build was slim, but strong; he did not strike as being the least handsome, but Diana, having grown up with him, found his looks comfortable and reassuring.

At the house, Gilbert left his horse in the stables and walking round to the front door was admitted by Corinne who had seen his arrival.

'Gilbert, I am so glad you have come, there is so much to tell you, but you will have to wait for Diana; she has ridden down to the village to see Annie Netheroyd. Such excitement, Gilbert, the new owner has been here — I am to call him Randolf, he says — and it is all signed and sealed. He is to put in the cropping frames and Diana is not at all pleased, but Papa says that it is progress. What do you think about it, Gilbert? Do come in and I will order some wine for you, perhaps I will have a glass, too.'

He followed Corinne and thought — not for the first time — what a very pretty little girl she had become. No, not a little girl any more, he told himself, a fetching young lady. He accepted that Diana would make him a suitable wife, but it was the little Corinne who appealed to his fancy.

'You are looking very pretty this morning, Corinne.'

She gave him a brilliant smile. Gilbert had always been a favourite with her, but he was bound to Diana. Now, of course, Randolf had appeared on the scene, but although she had been taken with him, she found herself somewhat in awe of the new master of the mill.

'You are trying to flatter me, Gilbert, this is one of my very oldest muslins. But you have come to see Diana about the frames, I expect, such a to-do. I think she quarrelled with Mr Staines — Randolf, that is — about it all. He is very handsome, you know, I am quite taken with him, but I think he is more Diana's style . . . oh, I should not say that for Diana belongs to you.'

Gilbert was amused. 'Is he not married then?' he asked her.

'No, he is not, but I suppose he is too old for me, I think he must be nearly forty.'

'Perhaps he would be good for you,' he remarked, still amused. 'He would probably help you to grow into the sensible young lady that Diana is.'

Corinne frowned. 'I don't think that I will ever be sensible as you put it. Would you prefer it if I was?'

He shook his head. 'No, I like you just as you are and soon you will be my dearest sister.'

'I think I would rather be your wife than your sister, Gilbert.'

'Corinne,' he rebuked her. 'Will I ever cure you of your unfortunate remarks? Let us talk about the cropping frames.'

Again the frown, but his time very serious. 'It is bad, you know. I listened to Papa and Diana talking about it. A lot of the village families will be badly hit if the men are put out of work. What do you think about it all?'

He was silent, surprised by her sudden seriousness. 'It is natural to want to improve things. I know that, for all the time I am trying to improve the quality of the wheat, to breed stronger lambs, but none of that affects my farmers and the men who work on the farms.

'With machinery in the mill, it is different. It might make more cloth and line the master's pockets, but that is at the expense of the well-being of the workers. Their families have to eat and it is hard when the man of the house is taking no wage home . . . but listen, that sounds like Diana now, we will soon learn if she has any news from the mill.'

Diana had seen Gilbert's horse in the stables and was not surprised to find him talking to Corinne. 'Gilbert, I am pleased to find you here,' she said as she greeted him in the drawing-room.

He politely and very correctly bowed over her hand. 'Corinne has been telling me of the visit of the new mill owner. I have yet to meet him, he seems to have made an impression on her.'

'He made an impression on me, too,' Diana replied. 'It was not a good one, I am afraid to say. It will cause distress in many families in the village.'

Diana sat in her usual chair by the fireplace and turned to Gilbert who had placed himself on the ottoman in the window. Corinne sat at his side.

'Gilbert, I have not discussed the

subject with you, I had hoped it would never arise. But the impression I have of Mr Staines is that he is a very forceful and determined man. He believes that to crop the cloth with the new machines will be more efficient. He is determined on it and I do not think that anyone or anything will make him change his hand. What is your view?'

'We must have progress, there is no doubt about that. If there had been no progress in the last century, the weaver and his wife would still be working in their cottages and there would certainly be no Keld Mill.

'When this wretched war with France is over, there is going to be a tremendous demand for good cloth and the best cloth in the world comes from the West Riding of Yorkshire. That is not just my opinion, Diana, it is a fact.'

She nodded, but her expression was obstinate. 'I do know that, but if it cannot be made without causing hardship to the workers and with no food for the children, how can we call it progress?'

'The time will come when there is such a demand for our cloth that there be work for all.' Gilbert spoke smoothly and succeeded in annoying his intended wife.

'I can see that you will get on very well with Mr Randolf Staines,' she said shrewishly.

'I will be keen to meet him certainly,' he replied.

She smiled at him; it was good to see and talk to the calm and sensible Gilbert and she hoped for no awkwardness at her next meeting with Randolf Staines.

3

Two days after this conversation, Diana rode again to the village to see Annie Netheroyd.

As usual, she took the track slowly, looking about her as she rode quietly along. Around her rose the familiar moors, that morning showing a darkened face. It was a dull, cold day, the clouds were heavy and black and threatened rain. But Diana loved her moor in all its moods.

Holmby was still as she approached its cottages and houses, the smoke rising straight up from each chimney was both comforting and reassuring. Each family was being kept warm and there would be enough heat in the oven to bake the bread; a pan of good vegetables would be simmering slowly on top of the hob for their mid-day meal.

The smoke also rose straight up from

the mill chimneys; with little movement from the wind, it seemed to hang its heavy grey pall over the village.

In all this grey stillness, Diana's eyes was caught by an unusual movement and it came from the direction of the mill. The great stone building, the pride of her grandfather, stood three storeys high at the end of the village. The river ran swiftly past it before making a quieter journey across the lower fields towards Huddersfield.

The moor was not so high above the mill and a broad track was easily picked out, winding its way down to Holmby from Wakefield and Barnsley.

It was on this track that Diana's attention was fixed. She could see a slow movement downwards and her keen eyes picked out two very large wagons, each of them drawn by four horses. She could not see the contents of the wagons, but it was not difficult to guess what they were holding.

She spurred Chester on, knowing that in the yard at the mill, she would find Randolf Staines awaiting the arrival of his cropping frames. I cannot be wrong, she muttered to herself as she rode briskly towards the village.

She forgot Annie and made straight for the mill, wondering what she would find. Would dismissed croppers be lying in wait in order to vent their anger on the objects which were putting them out of work?

Down the village street, all was quiet and she reached the mill yard quickly. Everything seemed to be normal; the usual rattle and deafening noise of the heavy machines driven by steam, the yard deserted because all the workers — men, women and children — were all inside the mill.

Diana saw Randolf immediately. Standing tall and upright at the counting-house door, he was a commanding figure in black coat and grey breeches, his hat almost hiding his dark hair; only his waistcoat showed any colour and it was an unusual cloth of bright green.

She thought he was alone, then she saw the familiar figure of Samuel Topping, the head overlooker, come out from the counting-house and take his place at his master's side. They did not converse and she could see a tense anxiety in their waiting pose.

She rode up to them and saw Randolf turn his head sharply at the sound of a horse on stones.

'Devil take it,' he swore loudly as she jumped down and went up to him. 'Diana Skelton, what in Hell's name do you think you are doing here? Begone quickly and I refuse to apologise for swearing at you.'

'Mr Staines, I can see wagons coming down the Wakefield road. Is it the cropping frames? Have you procured the frames already? You have lost no time in doing so.'

He was stiff with anger. 'What is it to you if I have the frames coming? You know my intentions and I want no interference from you or from anyone else you might round up to make a protest.

'The frames are coming in and the wagons will be here at any minute. I have no idea whether to expect trouble or not, but I am prepared. This is no place for a girl who is stupid enough to interfere.'

Ignoring his rage and his rudeness, Diana stood her ground. 'You are bringing misery to countless Holmby families all for the sake of a few extra pounds in your own pocket.'

'Be quiet,' he shouted at her. 'You know nothing of my plans, you know nothing of me. You might be the daughter of the previous owner of the mill, but to me, you are nobody.'

He stopped speaking and looked across the yard beyond the mill. 'The wagons are almost here, for God's sake go now. I don't know what will happen and I don't want you on my hands. Diana, do as I say . . . ' he turned to his overlooker. 'Samuel, you know Miss Skelton, for Heaven's sake persuade her to leave.'

'Miss Diana,' said the solemn Samuel

whom Diana had known since she was small. 'Best be off. Your pa would be shocked if he knew you was here. Expecting trouble from the men, we are, you be off like the good little girl you always was when I used to take you into mill and show you how looms worked. Please. Miss Diana . . . you know as it's dangerous.'

Diana took heed then. If Samuel said that it might be dangerous, then he was speaking the truth.

She said not another word, but jumped up on Chester and rode out of the yard quickly, but in time to hear Samuel's remark to Randolf.

'Never did need a hand up on that horse of her's, sir.'

'She's a damned little interfering fool . . .' came the echo of a reply.

Diana rode swiftly from the mill towards the Netheroyd's cottage.

She found Annie very anxious.

'Miss Diana, I'm that glad to see you. Such a lot of talk an' all. Zach hasn't said much, but he can't hide he's

48

fretting. There's rumours everywhere and I know he thinks as frames is coming. And he's up to something, I know he is, keeps getting together with other croppers, he does. But you'm bothered, I can see it. What is it, tell me worst. Have frames come?'

Diana nodded. 'It is not good news, Annie, I was on my way here and I could see wagons coming down the hill. I rode to the mill and Mr Staines and Sam Topping were both in the yard. Very tetchy, Mr Staines was, the frames were expected at any minute and I don't think they knew if there would be trouble or not. He sent me off and I've come straight to you . . .'

Diana stopped suddenly and looked round the crowded room; the table and chairs took almost the whole of the space, in the corner near the fire was the sold wooden cradle in which baby Netheroyd slept soundly.

She looked at Annie. 'Where are the children?' she asked.

'They've gone to their granny's. Me

mam knew I were worrying about goings on at mill and she said she would have them for the day. Small Zach and Georgy have gone to mill as usual . . .'

Diana interrupted. 'I've got a plan to help you . . .' but she could not finish as the door burst open so violently that she felt frightened and put out a hand to Annie.

The door was slammed shut and there stood the large man who was Zachariah Netheroyd. He was always known as Zach. He was big in all senses of the word; very tall, with broad strong chest and thick around the middle. His round face was topped by a mass of dark hair and his beard was long and busy; his smile was also big for he was naturally a cheerful man, beloved by his family, respected in the village.

There was nothing cheerful about Zach that morning; a heavy frown showed his anger, his mouth was set in a grim line. 'He's done it, the swine!' He shouted rather than spoke. 'Four cropping frames in, and over thirty of us with no work. He'll help us, he said, all posh like, but what can he do to help likes of us?' Annie was sobbing. 'You stay quiet, woman, and get bairns from their gran's.'

He turned to Diana. 'I ain't sorry for what I've said. All these years, we've worked for your pa and respected him we have. You stay with missus awhile, she'll be glad of your company. I'm not staying here, I won't come to no harm so don't you worry yourself. I'm doing what's right and no more.'

And with these words, he was gone and Diana heard the gasp of a sob from Annie.

'Oh, Miss Diana, it will be trouble, I know our Zach. He's made up his mind, you can see it, can't you? Can you do owt to help us?'

Diana tried to be practical though her mind was racing with a thousand ideas. 'Sit there, Annie, and stop crying. I will do what I can. But first, I will fetch the children from their grandmother's,

51

they will help to take your mind off whatever Zach might be up to.'

She left the children with Annie then stood outside the cottage in deep thought. Only her hand tight on Chester's reins indicated the tensions within her. She felt that her mind was a battlefield. Should she go straight back to the mill and find out what had happened when the frames had been delivered?

Should she confront Randolf Staines once again and ensure that he would do something to help the men he had dismissed? She did not relish a passage of arms with him and she decided on her third and easiest option. This was to go to Cannock Hall and seek out Gilbert; she could rely on his opinion and his common sense.

* * *

The Dyke family had lived near Holmby for centuries and the old hall, its grey stone not yet blackened by the smoke from Keld Mill, overlooking the village. Mrs Dyke had seen Diana approaching and was standing at the door to greet her.

'What news, Diana?' she asked quietly. She was a lady of fifty years, but looked younger.

'It is not good, Mrs Dyke. I was riding down to the village and I spotted what I thought to be the frames being brought down the hill. Sure enough, when I went to the mill, Mr Staines was standing in readiness. He sent me off very rudely, so I thought that I would come and see Gilbert. Do you know where he is?'

'He went up to the top moor. They are busy with the lambing, it is always later up there. I expect you will find him at the Wilshaw's farm. But, Diana, you know very well that you will find Gilbert in favour of any progress that the new master might want to make? He is always trying new ideas for better sheep or oats and a bigger yield of turnips of something like that.'

'But I cannot believe that he can be in favour of families not having enough to eat,' said Diana.

'You will see what he has to say, my dear, but would you prefer to wait until he comes home?' Diana shook her head. 'Thank you very much, Mrs Dyke, I think I would like to go and meet him. I am afraid that I feel rather agitated with all that is happening; a gallop up to the moor will do me good.'

She did have her gallop and was fortunate enough to meet Gilbert as he came away from the Wilshaw farm; she paused as she saw him riding towards her.

'Diana.'

Her name brought her back to her reason for being there and she greeted Gilbert. Then, dismayed with herself, she found herself comparing his pleasant and polite features with the handsome, fearsome rage of Randolf Staines.

'Gilbert, I have come to find you.

The cropping frames have been delivered to the mill.'

His reply astonished her. 'Good,' he nosed in approval. 'Staines will be pleased. I met him yesterday, he told me of his plans. I trust there was no trouble?'

'You agree with Mr Staines,' she said accusingly. 'You told me that you were on the side of the men who are put out of work.'

They were standing outside one of the stone barns that were dotted about the moor; the sky had darkened and Diana could feel a slight drizzle in the air.

She took no notice as she awaited Gilbert's reply and when it came, his lack of sympathy with her views annoyed her.

'Come into the barn, Diana, you are going to get a wetting.'

She gave a scowl, but they led their horses into the empty barn.

'Now, Diana, I do not want to quarrel with you. In a few months time, you will be my wife. I want a biddable wife and I have always regarded you as having that quality.'

She stared at him; his expression was unsmiling and bland at the same time, he showed no emotion. This was never the man she had agreed to marry, she was thinking furiously, and said the first thing that came into her head.

'If you want a biddable wife, you would do better with Corinne.'

A strange expression crossed his face and she could not guess its meaning.

'Perhaps that might be a good idea,' he said bluntly.

'You don't mean it, Gilbert?' Diana suddenly panicked. She did not love Gilbert as she had always imagined she would love the man she was to marry, but he was the last chance of her becoming a wife and she looked forward to being mistress of Cannock Hall.

He managed a smile. 'No, I don't suppose I do. I am fond of Corinne, but she is very young and it is you I have chosen to become my wife. Let us not quarrel. We will not always agree, but I certainly do not have words on the subject of the new master's cropping frames.'

'They are very important to me,' she said obstinately.

'We will leave the frames out of the argument and concentrate on what to do for the unfortunate men who have been put out of work.'

Diana was glad to have the vexed subject of the frames changed and she nodded. 'I am going to speak to your mother and to the Rector's wife to try and supply the families with oats and perhaps some vegetables.

'We might also raise a fund for the out-of-work men to take a wagon over to Barsnley to fetch some cheap coal.

Gilbert nodded. 'That seems admirable.'

Diana gave a sigh of relief at having the disagreement over. 'Thank you, Gilbert. Perhaps, if the children are fed, there will be no trouble, though the men are very independent and proud of the wage they have been taking home. It is no wonder that they try and destroy the machinery which has taken their work from them.'

She saw Gilbert bristle — it was the only word she could think of to describe his stance and the expression on his face. 'I do not wish to hear any talk of destroying machinery, Diana. It is wrong and it brings violence with it. Men are hurt and we must hope that nothing of the kind happens here in Holmby; and if there is any trouble, I don't want to see you taking any part in it.'

Diana frowned and then said the wrong thing. 'I think Zach Netheroyd is up to something according to Annie.'

'It is not right, Diana. Mr Staines will have put in the frames to improve his production, to increase it and all for the good of the mill. You cannot go against progress. We wouldn't have Keld Mill at all if it hadn't been for the invention of the power loom. You seem to forget all that.'

Diana could feel herself getting angry. 'You are not right, Gilbert, you and Randolf Staines between you. Thinking of your own pockets instead of the children having enough to eat. I know it's wrong. And if you think it's right, then I don't want to marry you. You can have Corinne if you want her.'

'Diana . . . '

But she had gone, rushing out of the barn into the rain which was now falling heavily, flinging herself on to Chester and galloping back to Keld Head House. She knew that she had been wrong in losing her temper with Gilbert, but she had never felt so out of sympathy with him.

★ ★ ★

The next morning, Diana busied herself by visiting Mrs Gilchrist, the Rector's wife and between them, they arranged for a collection to be made for the coal.

Then she rode to Cannock Hall and

found that Mrs Dyke had bags of oats waiting to be delivered round the village. From there, she went to see Annie and Zach and found them arguing.

'Miss Diana, you'm come just in time. What am I to do with Zach lolling around here all day when he should rightly be at mill?'

'Don't worry, Annie, I've come to tell Zach that I need his help to take round some oats to all the families who have been hit by this sad business,' Diana replied with a grin.

But no smile came from Zach. 'It's charity,' he scowled. 'I don't want your charity, I want work. I can give bairns better'n porridge when I'm bringing home a wage. We might not live grand here, but I've always fed them proper. But you'm trying, Miss Diana, I'll say that. What is it you want me to do?'

The question sounded more reasonable and Diana was relieved.

'Mrs Dyke has some sacks of oats waiting for us at the Hall. This is what I want you to do, Zach, and I will come with you. Get hold of a small cart and we'll go over to Cannock Hall, load up and bring the sacks here. They can go on your piece at the back of the cottage and you can get someone to help you put the oats into smaller bags to deliver round the village. There's enough for each man who has been put out of work and they will all have families, I am sure of that.'

Zach was nodding. 'Ay, Miss Diana, you're right there, bigger families than us, some of them. I'll do it, Miss Diana. It's right good of you to arrange it all like, and I'm not churlish enough to say nay when it comes to giving a helping hand.'

She gave a sigh of relief. 'Then there is the coal, Zach.'

'Coal?' he asked. 'What's coal to do with it all?'

'The Rector's wife is making a collection so that some of you men can go over to Barnsley and buy some cheap coal. It will be poor quality stuff, but it will keep the fires in the cottages going. I am going to leave all that to you, Zach; asking the men and getting a wagon and horses, then taking it round when you get back. Can you do that? I will bring you the money as soon as it is collected.'

'You'm a one, Miss Diana, you think of everything. I can't say nay when you is doing so much to help us. Ain't I right, Annie?'

Annie gave a broad smile; she looked relieved at the change in Zach and thanked Diana again and again. Diana left them then, pleased with her morning's work, but knowing that there was still a lot to be done.

4

Diana knew that despite all her efforts, the one thing she had not done was to ask Randolf if he would help; that very evening she rode to Mill House only to be told by Mrs Buckden the house-keeper, that the master was away at the Cloth Hall at Huddersfield.

She felt a disappointment, then a surprise when he came calling at Keld Head House the following evening.

Dinner over, she and Corinne were sitting quietly at some tapestry in the drawing-room when the master of Keld Mill was announced.

'Randolf,' cried Corinne as he entered the room. He looked striking in a dark blue coat, grey breeches and a plain white waistcoat.

'Corinne,' was all he said and made a bow. Then he turned to Diana.

'Diana, you wished to see me? Mrs

Bucken told me of your visit.'

Diana nodded. 'Yes, Randolf, there are one or two matters I wish to raise with you.'

'You sound serious.'

'I am serious,' she replied evenly.

'Shall we go into the library?' he asked and she sensed an air of remembered wickedness in his voice. She ignored it.

'Papa is in there. Would you mind walking in the garden? It is not cold outside?'

He shook his head, completely ignoring Corinne who looked aggrieved. 'The garden it shall be.'

Diana did not think that she needed her pelisse and picked up a shawl to put round her shoulders in case of evening chill.

'Shall we walk down to the beech trees?' she asked Randolf as they stepped outside.

'Is there nowhere we could sit?' he asked politely.

She looked surprised, but gave a

slight nod. 'Yes, there is the wooden bench in the shrubbery at the side of the house. Papa put it there because he thought we would be more sheltered when we wanted to sit out of doors. It is very pleasant there at the moment because some of the shrubs are in flower. Will that suit you?'

'It will suit me very well, thank you.'

She glanced up at him. 'You are very polite.'

'Do you think me incapable of politeness?' he asked.

'I am not sure,' she admitted. 'I hardly know you, this is only the third time we have met. Did you do well at Cloth Hall?'

'Mrs Buckden told you where I was?'

Diana nodded. 'Yes, she did. I know her very well.'

'I trust she was not indiscreet,' he remarked stiffly.

He is in a strange mood, thought Diana, I don't know quite what to make of him this evening. She gave a short laugh. 'Mrs Buckden might be talkative, but she is very trustworthy. You need have no fears on that score.'

They had reached the shrubbery, which, surrounded by a thick yew hedge, was indeed very sheltered.

Sitting with Randolf on the sturdy wooden seat, Diana felt an odd sense of intimacy. It was not an unpleasant feeling.

'Why did you come seeking me out at Mill House, Diana?' he asked her quietly.

I will be quite open and honest with him, Diana thought, even if it makes him angry. 'You must know that the families of the croppers you have dismissed will be in distressed circumstances if there is no wage going into the household. I wished to ask you if there was anything you could do for them.'

'Exactly what is your meaning?' he asked and his tone had an edge to it.

'I was thinking of other work which might be found for them or even if you could advance them enough money to live on until they can find work.'

'I have no money.'

She turned on the seat and stared at him. Dressed immaculately in a coat of the finest cloth, he did not give the appearance of being a gentleman without money. She could not understand him and said so.

'I do not understand you, Mr Staines.'

'Randolf, if you please, I do not like to be formal with you.'

'Very well. Randolf, how can you say that you have no money? You have just bought my father's mill. Only a rich gentleman could have done that.'

He did not reply. He got up and she watched him walk around the shrubbery; she felt certain that he did not see the bright red flowers of the quince bush or the white of her favourite viburnum. He was frowning and she guessed that he was pondering how to make his reply to her without losing his temper at her outspokenness.

He came and stood in front of her

and regarded her gravely. 'I have decided to be honest with you, Miss Skelton. I have never been a rich man and buying Keld Mill took my last penny. I am as poor as some of your croppers until I can make more and better cloth and find a good market for it.

'The fact is that I am so out of funds that my first mission had to be the journey to Cloth Hall to sell what cloth we had.' He paused and she thought that his expression was sincere and honest. 'I have no way of helping any of the families you speak of.'

Diana was astonished, and in her astonishment, she became angry, even rude. 'Randolf, you cannot be speaking the truth and for goodness sake, sit down. I cannot speak to you sensibly with you standing there glaring at me.'

He did sit down and started to speak. 'Diana . . .'

'No, let me have my say. You bought the cropping frames and you had no need to do that if you were penniless from buying the mill. You put frames in, you dismiss some of your men and then are not able to help them out, and you tell me that you are penniless. How can you call that progress? I daresay that I am being very rude, but you will soon learn that I am quite outspoken and try to reason things in a practical manner.

'My father has run the mill very successfully all these years without a hint of trouble even though they have been leaner years since we went to war with France. You arrive, and immediately, we are in difficulties.'

They were glaring at each other now; Diana sitting upright with her soft, brown woollen shawl round her shoulders, no hat or bonnet and with her rich auburn hair shining.

Randolf was admiring her beauty and her direct manner with him, but he was not going to say so.

'You look to the past,' he said. 'I look to the future. Keld Mill has been known for its excellent rough woollens and broadcloths, but my aim is higher than that. I want to produce the finest worsted; a cloth which all the gentlemen of Europe will want to wear because it is the best that can be found anywhere in the world.

'So I have to look forward. I have to look for an increase in production ready for when this dammed war is over and the European markets are open to us again.' He stopped speaking and noticed the intense concentration on her face. 'I have spoken at great length, but I hope that I have made you understand my position.'

Diana was silent; she felt calmer after her outburst and was surprising herself with a feeling of respect for the man who was now sitting at her side.

'You say nothing, Diana, did you understand what I said to you?'

'Of course I understood,' she snapped. How easily he can make me feel waspish, she thought. 'I would admire you if it were not for the poor families I am trying to help.'

'You are helping the stricken families? You yourself?'

'Yes, I am, does it surprise you?'

He studied her face. I thought her a surprising young lady when I first met her, he told himself, and it seems I cannot change my opinion. 'No, it does not surprise me. When I first met you, I thought you were the most beautiful girl I had ever seen.'

'Balderdash,' she snapped again, and this time with a heightened colour at his words.

'Then we quarrelled,' he continued as though she had not interrupted, 'and I discovered that you were a termagant. Now I find you helping those in need. You care, Diana, you really do care. Under your fine words and your accusations at my heartlessness, you care for these people of Holmby whom you have known all your life.'

She was startled as he put out a hand and stroked her cheek with firm fingers; then his fingers strayed to trace her lips and she trembled.

'I wish you would marry me. Cast off the admirable Gilbert, he is not your style at all. I met him, you know, he came to pay his respects on my first evening here. He may not have told you, it was very civil of him. But somehow I think he would do much better with Corinne, have you never thought of that? Shall I ask you again? Will you marry me, Diana?'

Diana found herself shocked at her feelings. This man was dangerously attractive to her; she had liked the feel of his fingers on her cheek and especially on her lips. If she had not been committed to Gilbert, he would have been tempted to accept the new mill owner even though, she thought wryly, life with Randolf Staines would be a tempestuous affair.

She forced herself into a spirited reply. 'You talk nonsense, sir, I believe I said so before. Gilbert and I are already planning our honeymoon to Italy.' She told the lie and wondered why she had made it. Perhaps it was because the new mill owner was indeed tempting to her. She heard him sigh and knew that it was feigned.

'Alas, I am too late. Do you think Gilbert would spare me a kiss?'

'There is to be no talk of kissing, if you please . . . ' Her attempt at protest was stopped by strong lips on hers; strong yet strangely gentle. She did not even pull away, she could not.

As the kiss slowly came to an end, they faced each other and their eyes met.

'Diana . . . ' her name was whispered.

'Randolf . . . ' she replied, then as he moved to pull her more closely to him, she came to her senses. This was Randolf Staines, mill owner, not Gilbert Dyke, the gentleman she was to marry. She must be bewitched. She stood up and walked away from him.

'We will return to the house,' she said stiffly.

'No, Diana, sit down a minute longer and I will apologise. Goddammit, I think you have me bewitched.'

He has even used the same word, she thought as she sat down again.

'Diana, I find that I cannot apologise for I enjoyed the kiss, except of course, it was not the behaviour of a gentleman. You must take it that the kiss came from your penniless bear of a mill owner. Now I must ask you something to take our minds from ourselves and our feelings.'

She smiled at his change of tone and tried to forget the disturbance of her emotions.

'What else do you wish to know?' she asked him.

'Tell me about Zach Netheroyd.'

'Zach? He is a good man to his family; he is rather a hot-head, but not a rabble-rouser, he is a proud man and very bitter at having no work. That is why I asked you to try and offer the men something. But it seems to be beyond your circumstances.'

'Yes, it is, I am afraid,' he answered her seriously. 'But I will give it some thought and I want you to promise me that if you hear any hint of rebellion or an attack on the mill, you will come and tell me. Are there any Luddites in the area?'

'No, not in Holmby,' she replied. 'There was trouble over at Rawford's Mill at Liversedge, but thankfully not in Holmby. I am sure of that. I know that Annie worries about Zach, but I think she would have told me if there had been any Luddite talk.'

'But you would let me know if there was any hint of trouble.' It was a blunt statement rather than a question.

She nodded, but said nothing more. Did he know more, she wondered? But she could not answer her own question and she rose and started to walk away from him. 'It is becoming cold and will soon be dark, I think we should return to the house.'

'Yes, Miss Skelton, certainly.'

Diana left him at the front door and went inside to an impatient Corinne.

'Diana, where have you been all this time? It is an age since you went outside and now it is nearly dark.'

'Randolf and I have been sitting in the shrubbery, we had a lot to talk about,' replied Diana, sitting herself near the fire for the walk into the garden had left her feeling slightly chilled.

Diana let one or two days go by before riding over to the Rectory to see how Mrs Gilchrist was faring with her collecting for the local coal fund. She found the Rector's wife very pleased with her efforts. The collection amounted to £50 and on the way home, Diana decided to call and ask Zach to organise the purchase of the coal.

She found Annie suckling the baby and Zach with his feet on the fender staring into the glow of a small fire. A good smell came from the pot simmering on the hob and Diana knew that although it contained only potatoes and vegetables, Annie would have added some herbs to it. She grew the herbs in the garden at the back of the cottage and the results was that their meagre dinner smelled pungent and appetising.

'You look gloomy, Zach,' said Diana as she greeted them.

He knew her well enough to make a straight and honest reply. 'Wouldn't you look gloomy, Miss Diana, with a wife and five children to feed and no wage coming in?'

Diana sighed as there was no satisfactory reply to this question. 'Never mind,' she said as cheerfully as she could. 'I have one piece of good news. Mrs Gilchrist has collected nearly £50 for the coal, so Zach, if you can find a wagon and get together the men who are willing to go, you can be off to the Barnsley pit in the morning.'

He turned to her at last and although he did not smile, he did look pleased. 'You'm a one as I'm sure I've said afore, Miss Diana. Not many things you can't set your hand to, no mistake. It'll give me something to do, what's more. I'll go round village this afternoon and get it all worked out with the men and we can be off first thing in the morning . . . ' he stopped as they heard a sharp rap at the door.

Diana opened it and to her astonishment, found herself staring into the handsome blue eyes of Randolf Staines.

He grinned. 'I thought as 'ow you was 'ere,' he said in his broadest dialect. 'I seen Chester outside.'

The colour rose in her cheeks. 'Don't you dare talk like that here, it is insulting,' she hissed at him and then turned to Annie who had hastily covered herself and put baby Netheroyd into the cradle.

'It is Mr Staines,' Diana said cheerily.

'Don't sound like 'im to me,' said Zach.

Randolf had come into the small room; his height and his presence seemed to fill it. 'I've come on a matter of business, Mr Netheroyd,' he said in his usual manner.

'I'll kill 'im,' muttered Zach, staring into the fire.

But Annie knew better. 'Get up,

Zachariah, the new master hasn't come for nothing.'

Reluctantly, Zach rose and faced Randolf. Both of them tall, and Zach the fiercest with his long beard and unruly hair.

'What is it then?' he asked and it was not said politely.

Diana saw Randolf look about him. He seemed to be taking in the simple poverty of the room which Annie had done her best to make comfortable and cheerful with colourful rag rugs and knitted cushions.

'How many children have you, Mrs Netheroyd?' he asked quietly.

'There's Small Zach and Georgy at mill, and Tom and Mary, they'm playing out back, and the baby here, it ain't easy, sir.'

Randolf turned to Zach who was still glaring fiercely. 'Mr Netheroyd. I am sorry that I had to dismiss so many of you when I put in the cropping frames. I am hoping that production will increase in time and that I will be able to take all of you back again.'

''Tis no good talking about future,' growled Zach. 'It's now that counts. Any fool can see that.'

'Zachariah,' said Annie sharply, but he ignored her.

Randolf continued as though there had been no interruption. 'I hope I'm not a fool, Mr Netheroyd. I want Keld Mill to become the best mill in this part of the West Riding.'

'That's as maybe. All right having grand ideas, ain't it, but what do I give bairns to eat? That's what I want to know.'

Zach spoke very aggressively and Diana thought that he would lose control of his temper — and his fists — very easily if he was provoked. She watched Randolf.

'I understand that and I have come to offer you some work.'

'What kind of work?' grunted Zach.

'I have a small garden at the back of Mill House and it has been sadly neglected with only Mrs Buckden living there. If you would clear it and get it dug over and some vegetables planted then I would pay you the same as you were earning as a cropper.'

Zach stiffened. 'You'm offering this to me? Just me alone? And what about all; them others, some worse off than me and Annie. We've got two lads working at mill for a few pence, others've got nothing. It's a damned insult to all us croppers. I ain't doing it. I ain't accepting your charity and you'd better get gone from my house quick afore I get nasty . . . '

'Mr Netheroyd . . . ' Randolf started to say, but Zach was on to him.

'Mr Netheroyd nothing, you mealy-mouthed pig, my name's Zach and always has been. Get out of my 'ouse and don't you dare put your foot round door again. Out wi' you, I say.'

Randolf put out a hand as though to pacify the irate man, but it was the wrong thing to do.

Zach's arms were up and his fists

were striking hard blows at the mill owner's head.

In the pandemonium which followed, Annie succeeded in dragging a shouting and cursing Zach away; Diana grabbed hold of Randolf's arm and pulled him towards the door.

'You are a fool,' she shouted at him. 'Or I am, I'm not sure which, I told you Zach was a hot-head. You had better go quickly.'

'You are coming with me,' he shouted back, putting his hand to his cheek which was bleeding slightly near the eye.

Diana turned her head back into the room; Annie had Zach sitting in his chair by the fire again, his expression thunderous. 'I will go with Mr Staines, Annie, and take care going over to Barnsley, Zach. I will try and ignore your violence and come and see you when you get back with the coal.'

Outside the cottage, Chester stood patiently waiting. Mr Randolf Staines was not so patient.

'Diana,' he said tersely and glowered at her as she took Chester's reins in her hands. 'They might be friends of yours, but Zach Netheroyd is a trouble maker, I am sure of it. I had thought it might help to offer him some work; it seems I was mistaken.'

'I have told you before, Randolf, your croppers are proud people. They prided themselves on getting such an excellent finish on the cloth; they not only worked long hours, they worked hard for a very low wage. But it was enough to keep their cottages warm in winter and to feed their children; they did not grumble at living such a simple life.

'Suddenly, it was all taken away from them, just from them; not the weavers, not the carders, not even from the children. They are united in their hardship and it was imprudent of you to single out just one of them and to offer him work.'

Diana thought she had said too much; his silence was threatening, but she knew in her heart that she must defend Zach and she continued without giving Randolf a chance to speak.

'Zachariah Netheroyd may be a hot-head, but he is loyal to his fellow croppers and I believe you can tell that he is a forceful and natural leader. I am sorry that he hit out at you, but you offered him an insult and it was his only way to react. I must hope that this incident will not lead him to taking any revenge on you.'

She stopped dismayed. 'I am sorry, Randolf, I have been reading you a lecture and it is not my place to do so. I am here to help the ones in trouble and in need. I shall continue to do so.'

Diana did not know it, but Randolf had been watching her with admiration. Her far from pretty face was full of a sincere earnestness and she emphasised each point with a shake of her head; her red curls had escaped her riding hat and tossed as she spoke with what he thought was a tantalising attraction.

I must get her away from that milksop of a Gilbert Dyke, he was vowing to himself, he might be a good friend to Diana, but he does not deserve her. I wonder if I can get him and little Corinne together, then the admirable Diana would be left for me.

'Diana,' he said evenly. 'I admire your rhetoric and I confess to believing you to be right. I happen to have other ideas for helping the dismissed croppers, but I cannot act upon them as yet. If you will be good enough to keep me informed of any unusual activities amongst the men, then I would be grateful to you. These are difficult times, but now I must be about the work of the mill and I will bid you good-day.'

He rode off on his horse and Diana watched him go. He is making trouble for himself, she thought, as she set off home on Chester. I fear for him and for the mill and yet there is something about him which demands admiration — she would have been amused had she known that Randolf had regarded her in the same light.

5

As she left the village and started up the hill towards Keld Head House, Diana heard the sound of a horse being galloped up behind her. She paused, looked back and saw Gilbert.

As immaculate as ever and on a fine hunter, she was left wondering why she felt such an impatience with him. She knew him well, he was kind, he was offering her a good marriage prospect, a fine home and yet that did not seem to be enough.

She knew that she liked him very much rather than loved him, but that had never bothered her. All this since Randolf Staines had arrived on the scene, she was reminding herself; yet she knew that more often than not, she was at odds with that particular gentleman.

'Diana, I am glad to find you at

home,' said Gilbert as he caught up with her. 'I wish to be private with you. Shall we walk round to the shrubbery and sit on the seat? We will be quiet there.'

They left their horse at the stables, walked to the shrubbery and as they sat together on the seat, Diana was reminded of the last occasion when she had sat there with Randolf. She gave an inward groan; I seem to be haunted by the mill owner, she thought, yet on every occasion I have met him, there seems to have been some prickliness or disagreement.

She gave her attention to Gilbert wondering why he had sought her out and thinking that it was probably the question of the honeymoon. In the stresses of the moment, she was not prepared to give it a minute's thought.

'Diana, I am aware that you have become acquainted with Mr Randolf Staines and that you are concerned about the welfare of the dismissed croppers and their families. On the occasion of our last meeting, you did not seem at all sympathetic to my plans, you could only talk about the affairs of the mill.

'I know that I disapprove of your involvement, but I do sympathise with Staines in his attempt to increase his production. It is something which is dear to our hearts whether we are farmers, land owners or masters of a woollen mill.'

Diana looked at him; he was not only very serious, there was a look of concern in his eyes which was unusual. He was always pleasant-natured and his estate was so well-managed that he seemed to avoid any pitfalls or worries.

'Something is bothering you, Gilbert?'

'How did you know?' he asked, genuinely puzzled.

'I thought you were looking worried,' she replied calmly.

'Yes, you are right; something has happened and although I know that we had words on the subject a few days ago, I think I would like to discuss it with you.'

Not the honeymoon, she thought, it cannot possibly be the honeymoon.

'What is it?' she asked with some curiosity.

'You told me that Mrs Netheroyd had said that she was worried about Zack. Is that right?'

She nodded. 'Yes, he is in a very aggressive mood and I have the feeling that trouble is brewing.'

'That was my feeling, too, and now I have learned something which seems to confirm it.'

'What is it, Gilbert?'

'I was up at the top farm this morning and had a word with one of the shepherds — Owd Bob, we call him. He told me that there is gossip going around that some of the dismissed croppers are planning to attack the cropping frames and he mentioned Zack Netheroyd in particular . . .'

'Why are you telling me this?' Diana interrupted sharply. 'You told me to steer clear of any trouble there might be over Randolf Staines bringing in the frames.'

'Yes, my dear, I do know that, but you are acquainted with Mr Staines and I am not; I have met him once and that very briefly when I called to make my respects on his arrival. But I want to ask you if you think I should tell Staines about it all. I feel that it is right that he should know.'

Diana smiled suddenly. 'You are a good man, Gilbert. Would you like me to go and see Randolf for you?'

'No, no, of course not. I do not wish to involve you at all. I simply want to know if you think that I am worrying unnecessarily, you are closer to the situation than I am. If there is any truth in the matter then I will go and see Staines myself.'

'Yes, I agree with you that Zach is up to something, but I know nothing about it. I think you should go and see Randolf as soon as possible.'

'You call him Randolf, Diana?'

'He asked me to.'

'I see, I hope I have no cause for jealousy.'

Diana tried not to smile. She wondered what Gilbert would have said had he known about the kisses; she, herself, could not forget them.

'No, of course not,' she replied. 'I think you will always find Randolf at home in the evenings, better to see him there than at the mill. I am glad you told me about it, Gilbert, I will be on my guard for any news. Now, are you going to join us for a luncheon? It is past mid-day.'

He stood up and putting out a hand, helped Diana to her feet. She could not but notice how quickly he took his hand away, almost as though he had committed a social indiscretion, she thought.

Then she told herself that she must not criticise a gentleman of such good intentions and correctness of manner.

'I would be delighted to stay, thank you,' he answered her. 'Will Corinne be at home?'

'Yes, I think so,' replied Diana, smiling to herself at the rather unexpectedly pleasant thought of seeing Gilbert and Corinne together.

Corinne cried out with delight when she saw Gilbert enter the drawingroom. 'I can guess that you have come to talk about the mill and I shall forbid it,' she told Gilbert as he took her hand.

Diana, noticing that he held on to Corinne's hand longer than was socially acceptable, and remembering his seeming correctness in the garden, began to wonder. I have a feeling, she found herself thinking, that Gilbert is more than a little fond of Corinne; there have been several small incidents recently which have caused me to think so.

What a pickle if it is so, she thought. Gilbert and I are to be married very soon and I am very fond of him, but no more than that. I have no idea how he feels about me, he has never spoken of his feelings. He seems to look to Corinne, but she would fall in love with any handsome young gentleman who paid her any attention, look at Randolf when she first met him!

Gilbert feels himself obliged to marry me so he cannot turn to Corinne; and what about me? Yes, I did look forward to being a wife to Gilbert and mistress of Cannock Hall, it would be hard for me to cry off even for Corinne's sake. But now, these little doubts keep arising.

I must forget it until the trouble at the mill is done with; what Gilbert has just told me seems to make it certain that an attack on the frames is planned. I think I will go and see Annie as soon as I can.

The next time Diana arrived at the Netheroyd's cottage, it was to find Zach at the back struggling with coal bags. A wagon was standing at the end of the piece; it was full of coal and Zach, with a curse and a swear and a shovel in one hand, was busy filling small sacks.

'Zach,' called out Diana. 'Is there no-one to help you? Where are the other men?'

Zach straightened up and faced her. 'Taken it into their heads to walk to Huddersfield, they 'ave, Miss Diana. Trying to find work there, but I ain't going. As I said afore, it's no life walking that distance at four o'clock in the morning and home again late at night. I'll wait and see what that swine of your'n comes up with.'

Diana looked at him; his expression was belligerent and she had the impression that for some reason of his own, he was refusing to go and seek work in Huddersfield. She did not voice her suspicions, but looked at the sacks he had already filled.

'You can't do all that by yourself, have you got the small cart ready?'

'Ay, it's in lane with pony, waiting.'

'Well then, go up to Keld Head House, it won't take you many minutes in the cart. Bring George and Henry back with you, they will love to help with filling the bags.' George and Henry were Diana's young brothers, usually to be found with their tutor.

Zach looked shocked. 'What would your pa say, Miss Diana? It's not right his boys doing work like this.'

Diana laughed. 'He won't know, he is up the clough at the small mills today. Go as quickly as you can, I'll be talking to Annie.'

He went off and Diana found a sober Annie washing clothes in a tub in the scullery; Zach had brought her water from the well at the corner of the street. It was used by several of the cottagers for drinking and cooking and for the washing if the rainwater barrels at the back doors were low.

'Zach's taking coal round today, Miss Diana, have you seen 'im?'

Diana told her about the boys and Annie was shocked. 'Whatever next, miss? But I'm glad Zach's got something to do, he wouldn't go to Huddersfield with them others.'

Diana spoke quickly, expecting Zach to return with the boys at any moment. 'Annie, I want you to promise me something.'

'What's that then?'

'If you hear any plans of the men attacking the frames, will you send one of the children up to tell me? Then I can go and warn Mr Staines. I'm not saying that what he is doing is right, but I don't agree with smashing the frames. Will you promise me that?'

Annie nodded. 'Yes, I'll do it, Miss Diana. It's hard with no wage coming in, but I don't want Zach or anyone else hurt if they start with fighting and there's no knowing that master might not call military in. That's what happened over at Rawford's, there were terrible shooting and two killed. We can't have that in Holmby, can us?'

'We will do our best to stop it, Annie . . . now I must go, I can hear Zach with the cart. When it is loaded with the coal sacks, I am going to drive him round the village.'

Annie was scandalised. 'You can't, Miss Diana,' she said and repeated Zach's words. 'What would your pa say?'

'Never mind that. I said I would help and I am going to help whatever anyone thinks.'

'You're as hot-headed as my Zach,' grumbled Annie, but Diana had gone.

Outside, she found two enthusiastic and excited boys, both of them carrying shovels; the coal was put into the small bags in no time at all and Zach sent George and Henry indoors to be cleaned up.

Then he found that he had Diana to contend with.

'Zach,' she said to him. 'You cannot go round on your own. I will help you deliver the bags to the cottages; put them in the cart and we'll be off.'

He straightened up and stared at her. 'You can't go deliverin' coal like a cottage woman, Miss Diana. I might be a rough 'un, but I knows what's proper.'

'Of course, I can help, Zach, we took the oats round, didn't we? I've got to help in any way I can.'

He still objected. 'I'm not having you carrying bags of coal, but if you could sit up front and drive pony, then I could nip into cottages easy like with bags. But your pa, Miss Diana, he'd be angered of you.'

Diana laughed. 'No, Papa approves of me helping out. He is very sorry about all this trouble since he sold the mill to Mr Staines. You fill the cart, Zach, and we will be off.'

Zach looked doubtful. 'I'm not sure on it,' he said, 'but I'll be glad of some help and that's a fact. But we can't put too many bags on, Miss Diana, or it'll be too heavy for pony. We'll come back for another load.'

Diana enjoyed herself. At each cottage, she was cheerfully received and by the end of the morning, she was thinking how hardy and courageous the mill people were. Never a word of grievance, only a heart-felt thanks to Zach and herself for taking the coal round. But by the end of the visits, she was tired of hearing the words 'whatever would your pa say'.

Diana drove the pony and when they

reached the cottage, she let the reins lie slack, climbed over into the cart and dragged the nearest bag of coal to the end where Zach was standing ready.

He took it on his shoulders and off he went into the cottage; it became obvious that he told the cottagers that Miss Diana was helping him for small children would rush out and more than once, Diana heard the words 'coal lady'.

Oh dear, she would think, perhaps Papa would not be pleased, but it gives me a good deal of pleasure to be able to help with such a simple task.

Zach was as black as a sweep, and had Diana known it, she too had gathered her share of coal dust to her hands and face.

She was wearing one of her old pelisses of brown twilled cotton which had seen many years of wear; she always wore it when visiting the cottages and not wanting to be seen *grand* or *stylish*.

They came to their last call, a very

small cottage standing apart from the others and was the nearest dwelling to the mill. It was, in fact, only yards from the counting-house in the mill yard.

Diana was helping Zach with his last load and he was off into the cottage when there came a loud shout from the direction of the mill.

'Diana.'

Diana, still in the back of the cart, straightened up. Only one person would have shouted her name so piercingly and in such an irate manner. She looked towards the counting-house to see Randolf striding towards her. She did not move.

'What in the name of God almighty are you doing, girl? Have you taken leave of your senses? Goddammit, you are Miss Diana Skelton of Keld Head House, not some town wench forced to do manual work. Come down from there immediately. What the devil are you thinking of?'

Diana did not move; she was standing still on the cart and held her head erect. She was not aware of it, but her bonnet had fallen back from her hair, her face was smudged with black and the hand she raised to flick back a fallen curl was as black as the coal she had been helping to deliver.

'Well, am I to have a reply?' The angry voice came nearer and Randolf stood looking up at her.

At the same time, Zach re-appeared from the cottage accompanied by three or four laughing children.

'Zachariah Netheroyd,' thundered Randolf. 'I might have known it, and what are the children doing?'

'We've come to see the coal lady,' they chorused and Zach, without saying a word, bundled them together and pushed them back into the cottage.

'Well, Netheroyd, what is the meaning of this?'

Zach was not allowed to speak, for by this time, Diana had moved to the end of the cart and had succeeded in jumping to the ground without assistance.

She faced the mill owner without flinching. 'Randolf,' she said with ridiculous superiority.

'I have been helping Zach deliver the coal to the unfortunate cottagers who have lost their work at the mill . . . '

She was quickly interrupted and Randolf's tone was scathing. 'Why, might I ask, could not the men I have dismissed helped in the task? It is beyond my understanding to know why a woman — notice I do not say a lady — should be required to do it.'

By now, Diana was angry, too. 'The woman was not asked to deliver the coal. She volunteered to help when she discovered that all the other men had walked to Huddersfield today to try and obtain work.'

'And Zachariah Netheroyd?'

'Zach was left on his own with the coal to bag up and deliver to the cottages. I offered to drive the cart for him to help him out,' she replied hotly.

'You will come straight into the counting-house with me and make yourself respectable. Have you any idea what you must look like?'

An imp of mischief entered Diana. 'I expect I look like a sweep, but I will come with you. I can hardly go home looking like this. I will just say goodbye to Zach and thank him for carrying all the coal.'

But unnoticed by either of them, Zach had quietly got up behind the pony and driven away down the street.

'Zach has gone, you wretched girl, you had better come and let me tidy you up . . .'

'I suppose you are going to say that you cannot imagine what my father would say if he saw me.' Diana was unable to stop the remark, but the reply came not as she had expected.

'I was not. Your father must be accustomed to your unfortunate behaviour. I was intending to say that I shudder to think what Mr Gilbert Dyke would say.'

Diana paused for a moment. Gilbert would not be best pleased, she knew that, but suddenly and somehow, Gilbert's opinion of her did not seem to matter.

At the counting-house door, she was greeted by a startled Samuel Topping. 'It never is Miss Diana? Why whatever's happened? Dang me if you don't look like you been down a coal mine or sweeping chimneys or summat . . . sorry, sir . . . ' he broke off as Randolf pushed him aside and shouted orders.

'That's enough from you, Sam; you will get warm water and some clean rags, and Diana, you will take off your pelisse and give it to Sam to shake out. Come into the kitchen.'

Without her pelisse and seeing her black hands, Diana suddenly felt in the wrong, but her thoughts were obstinate. Perhaps I was in the wrong, she thought, as she walked into the kitchen which she had known from her childhood, but what I did was right. Perhaps that sounds like a contradiction, but it was not exactly a crime even

104

if Randolf is behaving as though I have committed one.

Diana's dress under her pelisse, was of a green velvet cloth. High to the neck and with a row of buttons to the waist, it fitted closely to her figure and as she stood upright in front of the master of the mill, the soft swell of her breasts gave her a strong femininity which contrasted oddly with the disgraceful state of her face.

Randolf's manner softened in front of what he regarded as her bewitching presence. 'Diana, come to the sink, I will wash your face and hands clean for you.'

'Is it very bad?' she asked him.

He managed a grin. 'Let me fetch the mirror,' he said.

He held a small mirror in front of her and Diana almost laughed aloud except that she knew that Randolf did not consider it amusing.

Her bonnet hung down her back, her red hair was all over the place and her face . . . oh my goodness, she thought, no wonder Randolf is angry. Both cheeks were smeared black as though she had kept rubbing her fingers on them; there was a dark smudge on her forehead and her lips and chin varied between black and grey.

'Good Heavens alive,' escaped her lips. 'No wonder you were cross with me, I had no idea. I think I must have kept pushing my hair from my eyes and blacking myself at the same time. I can understand now why the children all wanted to see the coal-lady. Was it very bad of me, Randolf?'

He took a piece of white cloth in his hand. 'Let me clean your face up, then I will tell you.'

Diana had expected her face to be scrubbed fiercely, but his fingers were strangely gentle as he removed the black marks with the warm water. He wiped her lips last of all, then before she could turn away, he had bent his head and kissed her; at the same time, the hand which had been on her shoulder holding her still, slipped to

106

her neck and his fingers caressed the soft skin.

With feelings such as she had never experienced before, Diana stepped back from his grasp and looked around her wildly. 'Samuel . . . ' she stammered, but found to her relief that the kitchen was empty. Her temper flared.

'How dare you. If I have acted as no young lady should, then you are certainly not behaving like a gentle-man.'

'Diana, I was very angry with you, but I will confess — as neither of us are behaving as we should — that your body is very tempting to me. I will forgive the coal-lady if you will forgive the familiarity. You are very lovely.'

Diana was recovering her composure. 'Was it very dreadful going round with the coal? I only did it as an act of kindness as Zach had no-one else.'

'I will think of it as an act of charity on your part; fortunately no-one else saw you until you arrived at the counting-house. We will contrive to forget our misdoings, shall we?' His tone held a kindliness which surprised her.

'I hope Gilbert does not come to hear of it . . . ' she started to say. 'Oh, that reminds me that Gilbert wishes to see you.'

'Why should he wish to see me except to discourage me from admiring you too much?'

'Fiddle,' she replied. 'You are an infuriating person. I never know which side of your character you are going to show me next.'

'Which side do you like best?' he asked her and she knew it was in fun.

'I think it is the Randolf Staines who wants to improve Keld Mill,' she said thoughtfully. 'That brings me back to Gilbert. I believe that he wishes to speak to you about possible trouble at the mill.'

'Does he now? I wonder what he knows about it? I would be pleased to have an ally in the place.' He picked up her pelisse, shook it out again and helped her into it; then he took her bonnet and brushed it thoroughly before tying it under her chin. 'Now young lady, we will forget all this and get you back to Keld House. I gather you are not on Chester as you are in walking dress.'

'That is correct, I walked down today and in any case, I have to go back to the Netheroyd's to fetch George and Henry.'

'George and Henry?'

'Yes, my two young brothers. You have never met them for they are usually in the schoolroom.'

'But what are they doing at the Netheroyd's?' he asked her.

'When I found that Zach was trying to manage all on his own, I sent him up to fetch the boys and they helped him shovel the coal into the bags before Zach and I took it round.'

He stared at her. 'Whatever will you do next, Miss Skelton?'

'There is no need to say it like that,' she retorted promptly. 'The boys were very keen to help. I encouraged them.'

'Yes, I expect you did.' He put his hand on her arm. 'Perhaps one day I will get to know you. Let us go and fetch your estimable brothers, I suppose they will be as black as you were.'

'Annie will have cleaned them up,' she said. 'She is used to children getting themselves dirty.'

'Yes, I suppose she is. Off we go then. I think the main problem is going to be that if we have your small brothers with us, I will not be able to kiss you again.'

'Fiddle,' said Diana for the second time.

6

Randolf Staines and Diana walked down the High Street together and although few people seemed to be stirring, Diana guessed that there would be many eyes from behind curtains watching the new master and wondering at her walking with him.

At the Netheroyd's, she considered it unwise for Randolf to enter the cottage and she said so. 'Randolf, wait outside, the boys will be ready and I won't be a minute.'

He gave a wry grin. 'You are afraid that Zach and I will have a set-to,' he said.

'I'm not risking it,' she replied briskly. 'Wait there.'

A few minutes later, she joined him with two freshly-scrubbed boys who showed immediate pleasure at being introduced to Randolf.

'Mr Staines,' said George eagerly. 'You have had the cropping frames put into the mill. Can we come and see them?'

He regarded them both; they had the same intelligent alertness as Diana, and not ever having known Mrs Staines, he wondered how Corinne could be so different.

'Yes, you may come and see them one day, but not yet.'

'We don't like it when Papa says 'one day' . . . ' Henry started to say.

'It usually means never,' George finished for him.

'No, I will make a promise that one day soon, I will let Diana bring you to the mill to see the frames — or maybe your tutor would like to come with you.' He looked down at them. 'Whose side are you on, you young rascals? You are eager to see the frames, but here you are filling sacks of coal to help the croppers I have just laid off.'

George was very serious. 'It is difficult, sir. We find ourselves on both sides. We are keen to see progress in the mill, but recognise that it is very hard for people like Mr and Mrs Netheroyd. They have a family to feed and we admire Diana for trying to help, so we are pleased to help, too.'

'But we would still like to see the frames,' added Henry.

Randolf's eyes met Diana's over the boys' heads and both of them grinned. There seemed to be no answer to the question and at that moment the mill owner was unable to help.

'When I am sure that the frames are not to be damaged, you may come and see them working,' he told the boys. 'Now we are nearly at Keld Head House, you run on while I talk to your sister — and thank you for helping with the coal,' he added.

On their own at the gates of Keld Head House and watching George and Henry having a race up the drive to see who reached the front door first, it was Diana who broke the momentary silence between her and Randolf. He seemed deep in thought.

'You were kind to the boys, thank you. Am I forgiven for taking the coal round?'

He looked at her and spoke ruefully. 'I suppose so. There is no holding you and I think you would do it all over again if you were asked. Do you wish me to take you up to the house?'

She looked at him and there was laughter in her eyes. 'Thank you, Mr Staines, I think I can manage to walk the length of the drive on my own.'

'Shrew,' he said shortly.

'Maybe, but I thank you for cleaning me up and coming back with us. The boys enjoyed it.'

'You are fond of them,' he stated.

'Yes, very. It is almost as though they are my own sons and not my young brothers.'

'Perhaps we will have sons like that one day,' was his outrageous reaction to this statement.

As before, Diana lost her temper with him just when she was beginning to feel some accord. 'Why do you insist on such absurdities?'

'It is no absurdity,' he replied calmly. 'Is it something I hope for and like to think about when I am not entirely engrossed by matters of the mill.'

'How many more times am I going to have to tell you that I am going to marry Mr Gilbert Dyke? It is only six weeks away now.'

'Six weeks?' He was frowning. 'God-dammit, I will have to move quickly if I am to win you.'

'Bah,' said Diana, out of patience with him, and she started to walk quickly along the drive of Keld Head House, leaving a smiling Randolf watching her.

That evening, and well after dinner, Gilbert called at Mill House.

Mrs Buckden let him in and showed him into the library where he found Randolf sitting at his desk. The mill owner rose when he saw who his visitor was and stretched out a hand to him.

'Oh, Dyke, I was expecting you.

Diana told me that you wished to see me. Take a seat by the fire and I will bring you a glass of brandy, I am sure that you will not refuse.'

'Thank you very much, Staines, most acceptable. I felt that I must come and speak to you about some information I have learned that there might be trouble over the new cropping frames you have put in.'

The library was not a large room and was lit only by a four-branched candelabra which stood on the desk; the two men sat in armchairs in front of the fire and at that moment were facing each other gravely.

'Good of you to bother, Dyke, very good of you. I will admit to being prepared for trouble, but have no idea how or when it will strike. Perhaps you know more than I do.'

Gilbert told him the tale of his shepherd and the rumours about the frames and Randolf listened carefully.

When he at last spoke, it was seriously and carefully. 'It bears out what I have heard. Do you know the Netheroyds, Dyke?'

Gilbert nodded. 'A good family, but I believe Zach to be something of a hot-head. However, I understand he agreed to fetch the coal from Barnsley and has been taking it round to your croppers today.'

'Diana helped him.' Randolf made the statement deliberately to disturb the calm of this rather uninspiring gentleman.

'What do you mean?' came the quick reaction.

Randolf genuinely felt that Gilbert should know the truth in case there should be any gossip in the village, but he also had to admit to himself that he was hoping to rattle Diana's fiancé.

'I am afraid that your Diana went round with Zachariah Netheroyd this morning and helped him to deliver the coal; the other croppers had walked to Huddersfield to look for work so he had no-one to help him. Diana arrived at the cottage nearest the mill with a black face and the village children running out to the 'coal-lady' as they called her. I took her into the counting-house to get her cleaned up; she was not in the least penitent when I was angry with her.'

Gilbert gave a groan. 'Whatever will she do next? And our wedding only six weeks away, she will not even discuss any plans for our honeymoon journey. I say this in strictest confidence, of course. I never know what she is going to be about, though I will admit to her acting with the best of intentions. I am very fond of her, but there are times when I wonder if I really know her.'

'You don't love her?'

For an instant, Gilbert's expression was disturbed. Randolf could see on the face of the man he considered to be dull, a glimmer of animation which seemed unusual. Then it was gone and Gilbert was replying to the rather important question.

'I do not consider that a romantic love is necessary to a successful marriage. I have known Diana all her life and we deal admirably together, or we certainly did until this business of your cropping frames came to disturb the peace of Holmby. I am not criticising you for putting them in, Staines, for I believe in progress, Diana knows that.

'Once the men have settled down again, I think she will turn her attention to our personal affairs. As for love, it is easy to love someone who is not suitable to be one's wife and I firmly believe that a fondness and a regard are the most important . . . ' he stopped suddenly as though his thoughts were far away from the library of Mill House.

Regarding him, Randolf came to the conclusion that the gentleman he regarded as a dull dog was in love with someone else who would not make him a suitable wife.

Poor Diana, he said to himself, I will see what I can do; but there are more serious issues at stake and I must try

119

and find out if I can enlist Gilbert Dyke's help.

'Thank you for coming to tell me of your suspicions, I believe them to be correct. I will ask you if you would kindly come and tell me of anything else you might hear, in particular if there is any talk of a raid on the mill. I have made some preparations and I will need all the help I can get.' He paused and there was a silence between them.

Then he continued. 'The problem is that I don't know when it will come or how it will come. If I travel on my own, I carry a pistol; if it is not myself they are aiming at, then it must be the frames and I am prepared to defend the mill. I will tell you because I trust you and I think you will help me. I have a couple of Redcoats standing by, but I hope that it doesn't come to having to having to use force.'

'Does Diana know?'

'About the military? No, she does not. I don't trust her not to attack the frames herself.' Randolf was grimly serious as he made the remark.

'Good God, Staines, Diana would never do a thing like that. She is a lady.'

Randolf gave a laugh. 'You would not have thought her a lady if you had seen her with Zach and the coal cart this morning. She allies herself to the cause of the croppers too much for my liking even though she says that she is opposed to violence.'

'You alarm me, I will have a word with her,' said Gilbert. His voice was worried.

'Say nothing to her, if you please. I am grateful to you for coming to see me tonight and I will ask you again to be sure to come to me at the hint of rebellion.'

'Yes, of course I will, it is all very shocking. I thank you for your care of Diana this morning when she disgraced herself with the coal cart.'

Randolf smiled as he remembered the scene in the kitchen of the counting-house and how tempted he had been by her body. When all this is over, he told himself, I will look into the affair of Miss Diana Skelton and Mr Gilbert Dyke and see what can be done to prevent such a disastrous match.

Next day, Diana was thankful to see the other croppers back in Holmby and willing to help Zach deliver the coal; a few more journeys were made to Barnsley until each family had enough coal to last them for the winter. Warmer weather was on its way and the fires in the cottages could be kept low for the stew pot and the kettle; they would only need to be built up on baking days.

She went round the village each day with eggs and what vegetables she could find; May was a bad month for vegetables with last season's crop nearly finished and only a few parsnips still in the ground.

She had enjoyed taking the coal round with Zach, but had afterwards realised that it was not a proper thing for her to have done.

Her actions and appearance had produced what she had considered lecherous behaviour on the part of Randolf and this was to be followed by a quarrel with Gilbert.

He arrived at Keld Head House early in the morning after the episode of the *coal lady* as it amused Diana to think of it. She very soon discovered that Gilbert was not in the least amused; she had never seen him so angry, indeed, she had never seen him so animated.

She was getting herself ready for a walk to the village when he arrived on horseback and she greeted him at the front door.

'Hello, Gilbert. What brings you in this direction first thing in the morning?' she said cheerfully while at the same time thinking that his expression was rather disapproving. 'I was just on my way to the village. I have some eggs to take round.'

'I would like to speak to you, Diana.'

'Yes, of course,' she replied, wondering at his odd mood. 'Come into the drawing-room, I will just slip off my pelisse and bonnet.'

'Corinne is not here?' he asked when he realised that they were on their own in the room.

'No, she has gone with Mr Maidment and the boys to pick bluebells in Braythwaite Wood. We go every year, but I was too busy this year.'

'Too busy delivering coal, Diana?' he asked and there was an edge to his voice.

'You sound as though you object, Gilbert.'

'I do object.' He was standing close to her by the window, but he stared straight ahead of him. 'I object very strongly. While I admire your efforts to help the families of the croppers, I feel that delivering coal was taking it a step too far.

'It was not the action that any young lady should have taken, and certainly not the young lady who is to become the wife of a Dyke of Cannock Hall.

'What in God's name — and I make no apology for my language — were you thinking of, Diana? I understand from Staines that the other croppers were away seeking work in Huddersfield, but why could it not have waited until they returned? I fail to understand such disgraceful behaviour.' His voice was stiff with censure, but still he did not look at her.

I must try and keep the peace, Diana was thinking, but I will not apologise.

'It seemed the only sensible thing to do at the time,' she said calmly. 'I had George and Henry there to bag up the coal, but Zach had no-one to drive the cart, so I said I would drive it for him. There seemed no harm in that, it was the only way of helping out . . . '

Gilbert interrupted with some exasperation. 'But, Diana, if you were only driving the cart, how did you come to get so black with the coal?'

'I helped to put the bags on to Zach's back,' she said with some glee, then her tone changed. 'Who told you that I got so dirty from the coal, might I ask?'

'Staines told me when I went to visit him last night. I believe he thought he should tell me in case there should be rumour and malicious gossip about your behaviour. I was never more shocked. I suppose he must have found a maid to wipe your face clean or did you go home in that state?'

'Oh no, we were in the counting-house, he very kindly wiped all the black of the coal from my face.' I am making mischief, she told herself and for some reason, I seem to be enjoying it.

'Diana! What ever were you thinking of? Were you on your own in the counting-house with Mr Staines?'

'No I was not, Sam Topping was there, he shook out my pelisse for me while Randolf was cleaning my face.'

Randolf was not only cleaning my face, she thought, and felt a sudden sense of pleasure at the remembrance; he was holding me still and he kissed me, then I had to object to his familiar gesture. Poor Gilbert.

Gilbert suddenly turned towards her. 'Your behaviour is inexcusable in the lady who is to become my wife. I will have to ask you to stop going into the village with all your so-called good works. Your name will become a byword.'

'And if I refuse?' she asked him directly.

'I think I will not only be angry, but sorrowful at the same time,' he said and he was quiet.

Diana made up her mind suddenly. 'Gilbert, would you prefer it if I cried off from our engagement?'

He looked startled. 'Cry off. Whatever are you saying, Diana? Of course I do not wish you to cry off; our wedding is only weeks away now. Everyone would think I was ashamed of you for going round the village delivering coal.'

'But you are ashamed of me.'

'No, I am not ashamed. I just wish you to know that I do not approve of such behaviour and that I ask you most earnestly not to do it again.'

Diana smiled then. 'No, I will not do it again, Gilbert. I think I realise that it was wrong of me, but I shall take the eggs and the vegetables around. Surely you cannot disapprove of that.'

'It does not please me, but it is the kind of thing that good Mrs Gilchrist would do. If you wish to play the lady bountiful, I will not forbid it.'

How can I marry him, thought Diana, in a sudden panic. What shall I do? Then she remembered Mrs Gilchrist and Mrs Dyke and how much she admired them; she calmed down a little.

'Thank you, Gilbert,' she said very quietly. 'Shall we kiss and be friends?'

'What are you saying? I would never presume to kiss you before we are married. You are in an odd mood and I will leave you. I believe there will be trouble in Holmby before the week is out, so perhaps when all this business of the cropping frames is over and done with, you will consent to make plans for our marriage; after the wedding, it will be proper for me to kiss you, for then you will be my wife. Goodbye, and just one last word — do try and avoid any trouble at the mill, my dear.'

'Yes, of course, Gilbert, and I will tell Corinne that you have called, she will have been sorry to have missed you.'

'Dear little Corinne, you could do with a little of her sweetness. Please give her my love.'

'Yes, I will, Gilbert. Goodbye.'

He was gone and Diana sat down again; she did not know whether to laugh or cry. How can I marry him? What shall I do? She asked herself the questions and she did not know the answers.

Finally, she laughed heartily at poor Gilbert had he seen her with the coal cart; and she remembered. She remembered Randolf's fury, the gentle washing of her face, the kiss . . .

As soon as Gilbert had gone, she picked up the basket of eggs and walked down to the village; she made her way quickly round the cottages, making the Netheroyd's her last call.

She found Annie on her own with the children, Zach having taken the wagon for another load of coal.

'Oh, Miss Diana, did you get into trouble with master? Zach says as how Mr Staines saw you delivering the coal at that cottage near the mill; he says you was black from head to toe with helping with bags when you was only meant to drive cart. Zach came home and told me all about it, you shouldn't of done it.'

Diana smiled as she picked up each of the children and whirled them round, much to their delight. 'Neither Mr Staines nor Mr Dyke were very pleased, Annie, so I suppose I was in the wrong. But never mind, I assume that the other men are helping Zach today.'

'Yes, I think they've gone to Dodworth Pit this time, it's a bit nearer than Barnsley; just one last trip, Zach says, and you are not to come helping tomorrow . . . ' she paused. 'I hope as there's not going to be no trouble over cropping frames. Sometimes I wonder, but Zach, he don't say nothing.'

Diana was looking thoughtful and then spoke slowly. 'Annie, will you promise me something?'

'If I can, miss.'

'I know I have asked you before, but it is very important. It is Zach. If ever you have any suspicion that they are planning a raid on the mill, please will you send me word straight away? Send Small Zach up the Keld Head House, he's old enough to come on his own and give me a message.'

Small Zach was the Netheroyd's eldest boy and was twelve years old; he worked at the mill as a piecer, one of those children employed, because of their nimble fingers, to join broken pieces of thread.

Annie was nodding in agreement. 'I'll do that, Miss Diana, you can be sure on it. But what is there you can do?'

'I will be able to warn Me Staines as soon as I can,' Diana replied briefly.

'But he will get in Redcoats and only

the good Lord knows what will happen then.'

'Annie, I am sure I have said this to you before. I will do anything I can to help the croppers, but I do not agree with the violent smashing up of the frames. It must be settled some other way and I have confidence that Mr Staines will find that way. That is all I am prepared to say. Will you do as I ask?'

'Yes, miss, I will an' all. I'd do anything you asked, you'm that good to us.'

'That is all right then, Annie, I'll leave you now and both of us will keep our wits about us.'

'Yes, Miss Diana,' said Annie.

7

Not having seen Diana since their argument, Gilbert thought perhaps he had been too heavy-handed with her when he had censured her for delivering the coal; he rode up to Keld Head House first thing in the morning.

It so happened that Diana had been in a disagreement with Corinne at breakfast time and that she had ridden down to the mill hoping to see Randolf. She and Gilbert passed, both on their horses, within a hundred yards, but did not see each other.

Although the two sisters were so different, it was rare for them to disagree, but that morning, when Diana announced her intention of going down to see Randolf, Corinne was incensed.

'Diana, whatever will you do next? First it was delivering the coal and now you are saying that you are going to see

Randolf at the mill. It is not very lady-like of you. I don't know what Gilbert would say.

'Have you forgotten that you are about to marry him and your lovely dress made for you already? Mine, too, come to think of it, for it is quite the loveliest gown I ever had. You can't go to the mill to see Randolf, surely it is not that important?'

Diana had let Corinne have her say, but had taken little notice of her sister's protestations. She wanted to tell Randolf of Annie's fears and did not want to wait until he had gone back to Mill House in the evening. If it was unconventional that she should call on one gentleman while engaged to another, it did not worry her. These were not conventional times; she said so to Corinne.

'We are living in difficult times, Corinne. If it is not proper in me to call and see Randolf at the mill, it does not worry me. If it worries Gilbert, then it is his own misfortune.

He knows as well as I do, and as you do, that Randolf has stirred up trouble in the mill and in the village by putting in the cropping frames. It is up to us to try and prevent the croppers doing any damage.'

'Diana, you do not speak as Miss Skelton should, Gilbert would be ashamed of you.'

'Gilbert is ashamed of me, he almost said so. I offered to cry off,' stated Diana.

Corinne stared. 'You offered to cry off? You cannot be serious. Cry off from marrying Gilbert when he is the perfect gentleman and owns Cannock Hall? You must be mad.'

Diana was amused. 'Perhaps you would like to have Gilbert if you think him so perfect,' she said and noticed a flush come into Corinne's face.

'Of course I cannot have Gilbert as you so rudely put it. You know very well that the match was arranged by Papa and Mama and Gilbert's parents years ago. You were the obvious choice for him, I was far too young.'

'But you have grown up, Corinne,' said Diana.

'What if I have? I like Gilbert and I know that Gilbert likes me, but he has chosen you; that is rightly so. You should feel honoured, not talking of crying off. Do not tell me that you have fallen in love with Randolf.'

Diana rose in haste from the breakfast table. 'Of course I have not. What are you thinking? I have no patience with you. I am going to marry Gilbert, Randolf does not come into it. Do not forget, Corinne, that I am four-and-twenty and have no wish to remain an old maid.'

She paused at the door and felt herself remiss at her lack of patience with her young sister. 'I am going to the mill now and will see you later in the morning.'

She left the room and Corinne looked after her, an odd look in her eyes. I wonder, she was saying to herself, I wonder. If I could get Diana and Randolf together then Gilbert would be free to marry me and I would be mistress of Cannock Hall.

She gave a small smile of satisfaction and went into the drawing-room to take up the romance she was reading. The indulgent Mr Skelton kindly brought the books for her from the circulating libraries in Huddersfield and Leeds.

She was lost in her story and looked up with a start when she heard Gilbert's name announced. She rose quickly and went to greet him, she felt flustered and was not sure why; she had been welcoming Gilbert to Keld Head House for as long as she could remember.

'Gilbert,' she exclaimed as he took her hand. 'Diana is not here.'

'Has she already left the house? No doubt to do her good works in the village; I thought that if I came early I would find her at home. I am afraid I lost my temper with her, Corinne, and I have come to apologise. You were not here. I think that Diana said that you and the boys had gone to pick blue-bells.'

She nodded. 'Yes, we go over to Braythwaite Wood every year, but look, as soon as we put the flowers in water, they droop their heads.'

Corinne stood at the window next to a small table which bore a large vase of bluebells. her muslin dress was the same colour as the flowers and Gilbert could not keep back his next remark.

'You are looking very pretty this morning, Corinne. In fact, I think you grow prettier every time I see you. Suddenly you have become a very fetching young lady.'

Corinne smiled as she looked up at him. 'You must save your flattery for Diana, Gilbert, I understand you had a disagreement.' She sat down again and he pulled up a stool to sit at her side.

'Did Diana tell you?' he asked.

'Yes, she did; now she has gone off to see Randolf Staines and at the mill of all things. I thought it was most improper of her. I told her so.'

Gilbert leaned forward. 'She thinks only of the croppers' grievances, Corinne, and she is not behaving as the lady who is to become my wife should behave. Did you hear about the episode of the coal cart?'

Corinne giggled.

'It was beyond everything that was proper, but I am afraid that Diana does not heed the opinions of others. It is no wonder that you were cross with her, Gilbert. Now she has gone off to see Randolf. I told her it was not the correct thing to do when she is engaged to you.'

'She will come to no harm with Staines, he thinks only of his mill. But I do believe that Diana has little regard for convention, there are times when I despair of her. Why did I not choose you, Corinne?'

The question caused Corinne's colour to become pink, but her reply was quick and pert enough. 'Probably because I was only sixteen at the time and only just out of the schoolroom.'

Gilbert sighed. 'Yes, that is quite true and Diana seemed the perfect choice. Do you know why she has gone to see Staines and at the mill, too?'

'I think it was about something that Annie Netheroyd said to her; Diana went to see her yesterday.'

'I sympathise with Staines and I will help him if I can, but I don't want Diana becoming involved. Whatever is she thinking of now? I trust there will be no more coal deliveries.'

Corinne laughed. 'You are very good, Gilbert, I cannot imagine you losing your temper.'

'I don't think I would have cause to do so with you, young lady. But I will not wait for Diana to return, I have to go to one of the farms.'

He rose to leave the room and Corinne followed him. 'You are a good landowner, Gilbert,' she remarked.

'I love it,' he said and he took her hand in his in farewell. 'I am glad that you were here, Corinne, it has been very pleasant.'

Corinne watched him ride off and found herself sighing. He is such a good person, she was thinking, I do not suppose Diana knows how lucky she is.

Diana, in the meantime, had ridden into Holmby and decided to call at the Netheroyd's before going on to the mill to see Randolf.

She wanted to be sure that all the coal had been delivered and she also thought that there might be fresh news to take to the mill.

In the small cottage, she found a distressed Annie who was sitting by the fire rocking the baby in her arms.

She turned sharply as Diana let herself in the front door.

'Oh, Miss Diana, thank the good Lord you've come with me not knowing which way to turn next and I couldn't even send a message to you with Small Zach and Georgy being at mill . . . oh, Miss Diana . . .' and Annie broke down in a flood of tears.

Diana quietly took the baby from her and put him in his cradle, he did not stir. Then she put her arms round Annie and tried to speak soothingly.

'Dry your tears, Annie, and try and tell me what has happened. Where are the children and where is Zach?'

'Bairns are at their Gran's, thank God, been there all night, they have. Zach and them others are taking round the last of the coal. It'll take 'em all morning so I'm safe to talk to you. Yesterday, Zach were out all day over at Dodworth Pit, but in the evening, he went off again and I were suspicious. He went out back way, too, which weren't like him. So I crept out over the piece and there they were down back lane, Miss Diana . . . ' Annie stopped.

'Who were there, Annie? Did you know any of them?'

'Yes, I did, it were nearly dark, but I knew them all right. It were all them croppers who's been laid off, talking away in low voices, they was . . . oh, Miss Diana, I'm sure as they'm planning something, though Zach came back all bright and breezy and said as he'd been fixing cart as it weren't running proper. I knew it were a lie, didn't I, and it's not like Zach to lie to me. Do you think you should warn master?'

Diana did not hesitate. 'I will go and tell Mr Staines straight away. Then you must remember two things, Annie. First of all, don't tell Zach that I've been here, and the second is even more important. It is just as I told you before; if you think that Zach is going off to attack the mill, please send Small Zach up to Keld Head House with a message. Just to say 'Pa's gone' or something like that. I will know what it means and what I have to do. And I'll give him a sixpence.'

Annie smiled then. 'Miss Diana, you was sent to us by the good Lord, that I'm sure of, and I promise to stop crying and do what you tell me.'

Diana kissed her cheek, let herself out and jumped on the waiting Chester. At the counting-house, she found to her dismay that Randolf was not there and she tethered the horse and looked about her.

The great three-storey mill of which they were so proud was in front of her and even from there she could hear the clanking of the machinery; it seemed to shake the building. She decided to go in search of Randolf and she met him as he hurried down the stairs from the upper floor.

'Diana,' he shouted above the noise. 'What is it? Would it not have waited until this evening when I would have been at home?'

'No, it would not wait,' she shouted back. 'I consider it to be urgent. I must talk to you.'

'Very well then,' he sounded resigned. 'Come down to the counting-house, we cannot speak in here.'

She followed him across the yard and into the small building; they sat facing each other across the table which was littered with papers.

'You look worried, Diana.' Randolf was the first to speak.

She looked at him. He was dressed all in black relieved only by a grey neck cloth of linen, she guessed that he did not like to look flamboyant in front of his workers.

'I do not want to make a fuss about nothing, but some information has come to me which I thought you should know.'

'Are you working for me or against me, Diana?' She thought his tone prickly.

'Randolf, I know that I have been helping the croppers' families, I happen to think their need is very great. But at the same time, I have a horror of any violence. I do mean violence to people or to property, and of course, I mean the frames. I cannot object to them if they produce a better finish on the cloth, but I think it is a pity that other work could not have been found for the croppers.'

'Yes, ma'am,' he said.

'I know that we have been through all this before and that you are probably

145

losing patience with the Skelton girl, as I am sure you think of me.'

'It would surprise you to hear of how I think of you, Diana.'

'Fudge,' she replied. 'Let me say what I have come to say.'

'Certainly.'

'I have just come from Annie Netheroyd. Zach was not there as he was out delivering the last of the coal . . . '

'It surprises me that you are not with him,' he remarked sardonically.

Diana tried to keep her temper in check. 'Be quiet and let me have my say. I think you will soon realise how serious it is.'

'I promise to take you very seriously, Diana, but first, might I offer you a glass of brandy?'

'No, thank you,' she replied. 'I consider it to be a gentleman's drink.'

'As you wish.'

He is being very short with me, she observed. Is he worrying about the frames, I wonder? His face shows no sign of worry, it is just his manner. But I must tell him about Annie and Zach.

'Please listen carefully for it concerns you in a very particular way.'

'Do proceed,' he said.

'Thank you. When I got to the Netheroyd's this morning, Annie was in tears. Zach was out and the children were at their grandmother's, so Annie was free to speak. She told me that she had seen Zach and the other croppers meeting together after dark; it was in their back lane last night. Zach had lied to her about it and it made her suspicious that they were up to no good. She wanted me to come and tell you.'

He leaned forward and took her hands in both of his; she did not try to pull away as, for some reason, she felt that each was obtaining strength from the other.

'Diana, I want you to know that I appreciate what you have done, what you are doing. This is a clear enough warning to me and I know what I must do.

'I will tell you that before the day is over, I will have Redcoats at the mill. They have been standing by in readiness in case something like this should happen.'

'The militia?' she said fearfully. 'That means shooting.'

'You must trust me, my dear, I know what I am going to do and with the militia beside me, I hope to avoid any bloodshed. If the mill is attacked, then I promise you that I will try and bring the confrontation to a peaceful conclusion.

She looked at him, her hands were still in his and it gave her the confidence she felt she needed.

'You sound very sure, Randolf.'

He did not smile, but his voice was less strained. 'It makes things easier when we know what we are up against and I have to thank you for that, Diana. I just ask one more thing of you.'

'Yes, of course, Randolf.'

'If you have any more news or any information at all, please will you let me know as soon as possible. I will stay at the mill all night.'

'Yes, of course,' she replied readily and told him how she had asked Annie to send Small Zach with a message.

He squeezed her hands and stood up. 'Bless you, my dear.'

Outside the counting-house, they found Chester waiting patiently.

'May I hand you up?' Randolf asked.

'I usually jump,' she replied.

'Yes, I expect you do. I wonder you do not ride astride like a gentleman.'

'Bah,' Diana said and rode off without another word.

That evening at Keld Head House, Diana found herself feeling anxious as she wondered if Small Zach would arrive with a message.

She had lit only one candle in the drawing-room and had played a half-hearted game of backgammon with Corinne, as soon as they had drunk their tea, she had sent her sister upstairs to prepare for bed.

Mr Skelton was away in Leeds, visiting his sister and her husband.

Her intention was to draw back the curtains in the dimly-lit room and to stand in the window to watch the drive for Small Zach. It was almost dark now and she was sure he would soon be arriving with his important message.

The faint glimmer from the candle cast a pool of light on the gravel area by the front door; Diana strained her eyes, watching carefully for a moving figure.

She could see no farther in the murkiness of the night; even the lights from the cottages down the hill were obscured.

When it came, the knock on the front door made her start, for she had seen nothing. She heard the maid, Ellen, open the kitchen door and hurried out to stop her.

'Oh, Miss Diana, whoever would it be at this time o' night. I'm scared to answer the door, that I am.'

'Run back to the kitchen, Ellen, I will open the door.'

'Oh no, miss, I can't let you do that.'

'Do as I say and be quick about it,' snapped Diana.

'Yes, miss,' came the reply and Ellen was gone.

Diana opened the door carefully with no feeling of alarm, though it came as a relief to see a small figure standing there. 'Small Zach, I've been expecting you.'

'I came as quick as I could, Miss Diana,' said Small Zach.

'Come along in, I've got a sixpence for you. Have you got a message from your mother?'

'Yes miss. All I've got to say to you is 'It's tonight'.' Small Zach, clutching his cap, looked to see what reaction there would be to his message.

Diana felt a prickle of alarm which was almost excitement. She knew that she must hurry down to the mill to tell Randolf though she guessed he was prepared.

151

'Here's your sixpence,' she said to the boy. 'I am going to the mill, do you want to come with me?'

'Oh, yes please, miss, is there going to be trouble?'

Diana sounded calmer than she felt. 'Yes, I expect so. Wait there while I get my cloak.'

In the large entrance hall, she had left a long, black hooded cloak hanged from the rack. As she reached for it, Corinne's voice came from the stairs.

'Whatever is it, Diana? I heard a knock on the front door and then voices. Are you all right? Why are you putting your cloak on? Oh, and that is Small Zach, isn't it? Was it him at the door? Is it something exciting, Diana?'

'That's enough questions, Corinne, please go back to bed.'

'I am still dressed. You are never going out at this time of night, Diana.' Corinne had reached the bottom of the stairs.

'I have to take a message to Randolf at the mill. It is very urgent and I wish

to be off. Please don't detain me.'
Diana fastened her cloak and put the
hood over her head; she knew she
would not be recognised.

'Detain you?' echoed Corinne. 'I am
coming with you. Papa would never
forgive me if I let you go on your own.'

Diana was torn. She had no time to
stop and argue with Corinne and it
would not matter if her sister was with
her.

'Fetch your black cloak like mine,
then, and be quick about it. And
whatever happens, you are not to say a
word. You are to keep quiet. Do you
understand?'

'Of course I understand, do you take
me for a simpleton? My cloak is in my
bedroom, I will go and get it.'

Five minutes later, Diana, Corinne
and Small Zach were walking quickly
and silently down the dark drive of
Keld Head House.

8

On that dark, gloomy night, few sounds were to be heard by the three walking down towards Holmby. There was the occasional rustle of a small creature running into a hedge, the distant hoot of an owl, the scuff of their shoes on the stony lane. They did not speak.

Corinne and Small Zach were walking in front and Diana following them, lost in thought and with an uncontrollable feeling of fear. She did not know what to expect and walked with a premonition that trouble lay ahead. She was jerked from her thoughts by the sound of Corinne's high voice.

'Whatever is that glow over Holmby? It is near the mill. Look, Diana, surely they cannot have set fire to the mill.'

Diana could see what Corinne had spotted. From the direction of the mill, there was a soft halo of light, it was steady and more like a glow, as Corinne had said.

Diana shook her head. 'It is not a fire, we would hear the crackle and see the leaping of flames. I suppose it could be a crowd of protesters all holding a flaming torch, but I hope not as I wanted to get to Randolf in time to give him the warning.'

They hurried then, soon reaching the cottages and making their way round the backs, avoiding the main street. A path took them to the side gate of the mill.

Diana was to remember for ever afterwards the scene in the mill yard. The mill itself explained the glow in the sky, for in every window, on all three storeys, stood a lighted candle. The lights burned steadily and Diana guessed that they were doing exactly what Randolf had intended. He must have already received the warning which she was bringing to him, for instead of lying in grim darkness, the yard was bathed in light. Randolf had guessed that any attackers would have been relying on the mill being in pitch darkness.

She smiled then, but in the instant it took her to turn to Corinne, her smile vanished as a great crash came from the gates.

She caught hold of Corinne and Small Zach and drew them back to the shelter of the high wall which surrounded the yard. Unknown to them, as they had walked silently down the hill, Zach and the other croppers had reached the mill gates.

Diana watched anxiously and as she did so, a huge hammer was raised by one of the men and the locks on the gates were broken in one massive blow.

Both Diana and Corinne would have been hard put to have described what happened next for all was mayhem as dark figures surged into the courtyard and stones and rocks came flying through the air. There was a sound of shattering glass as many of the mill windows were broken.

Corinne clutched Diana's arm. 'There's Randolf . . . and Gilbert, too . . . oh, and here are the Redcoats.'

'Shhhh,' hissed Diana and watched closely. The door to the mill had opened and Randolf, and indeed it was Gilbert, stood on the step, then she saw the Recoats standing stiffly on either side of the two men. All carried muskets, Randolf and Gilbert, too, and Diana gave a hysterical giggle. Gilbert Dyke with a musket was a sight she would never have imagined.

On the other side of the yard, and just inside the gates, the crowd of men were threatening; a shout was heard and they advanced. Slowly and with a silent shuffle; the malice on their faces could almost be seen.

'Diana . . . ' whispered Corinne.

'Be quiet, be quiet, will you?' Diana put an arm round the girl; Small Zach stayed close to them saying nothing.

Randolf was speaking though it was more of a roar. He looked magnificent, Diana thought. All in black, even his breeches were as black as his boots, and as though in defiance of the mood of his men, he wore an elaborate neck cloth of pure white, the fall of which any dandy might have envied.

'Any man of you who takes as much as a step forward will receive a warning shot. I do not seek violence, but I am prepared to defend the mill to the last.'

He stood stiff and straight, as did Gilbert, and Diana felt a thrill of pride. Yet her eyes were on the shifting tide of men, their stones were spent, they were waiting for the next orders. Diana knew that somewhere in that dark crowd was Zach Netheroyd, ready to take revenge for not being allowed to provide for his family. She kept a tight hold on Small Zach who was watching with the same intensity as she was.

There seemed to be a long, tense moment of stand off; the Redcoats with their muskets primed were ready. Randolf was still on the alert, Gilbert not moving. Diana held her breath in an agony of waiting. Waiting for someone to move? A shot to be fired? She continued to hold on to Corinne and Small Zach.

Then it came. A dark figure breaking from the crowd and making a dash for the mill door.

A shot rang out.

The man was thrown forward and a roar went up.

But over the roar came the shrill voice of a child.

'It's me pa, it's me pa . . . '

The cry came from Small Zach and with it he wrenched himself from Diana's protective grasp and ran forward to the still figure.

At the same time, and to Diana's everlasting shame, there was heard another voice. It came from her sister.

'No, Small Zach. Come back, come back, you will be shot.'

Corinne tore herself away from Diana as Small Zach had done and ran quickly to the boy kneeling beside the man who had fallen at the shot and was now rising to his feet.

A small figure she was, and as she ran in her black cloak, the hood fell back and revealed her fair, golden hair.

At the same time, another short rang out and Corinne fell with a cry and a scream.

Pandemonium then. Randolf yelling to the Redcoats to fire into the ground if anyone moved, then walking down the yard to confront his workers.

'Don't move, not any one of you. Stay where you are,' he yelled.

Diana ran to the fallen Corinne and found herself confronting a Gilbert who was taking her sister into his arms.

'My little love,' he said. 'Speak to me.'

Diana watched with an amazement which seemed to her to be a fleeting second of glorious joy as she heard Gilbert's word to Corinne.

'Gilbert, Gilbert, it is you,' cried Corinne. 'It is my leg, Gilbert, my leg. Nothing more, but I can feel the blood . . . oh, Gilbert, I was only trying to stop Small Zach.'

But it was Zach and not his son, who spoke. 'Miss Corinne, you shouldn't 'ave moved. I threw myself to the ground to miss being shot, I ain't hurt. But I 'ad to get into the mill, Miss Corinne, I just 'ad to.' Then he seemed to realise that Small Zach was standing there and he put his arms round his son. 'What are you doing 'ere, son? It's not the place for children.'

No-one listened to him.

Diana had lifted Corinne's cloak and dress and found the wound in the flesh of her leg below the knee. It was not a bad wound, but it was bleeding profusely.

Gilbert acted quickly. They could hear Randolf shouting and the uneasy shifting of the crowd. But Gilbert tore off his neck cloth and bound it tightly round Corinne's leg.

'My love,' he kept saying and Diana looked at him in astonishment. Then he turned to Zach. 'Carry her into the counting-house, Zachariah, and be careful with her. Lay her down on the settle. And you, who seem to be Zach's boy, run down the village for Mr Pennycross, the sawbones, he must come and take the ball out. Diana, go with her and give her some brandy, Randolf keeps some there. I will be with you as soon as I can. Have courage, my foolish little one,' he said to Corinne.

In the few minutes it had taken for this incident to take place, Diana had stood by in bewilderment. How could Corinne have behaved so stupidly? And with Zach not hurt at all.

What was the meaning of Gilbert's strange behaviour, his words, his gentle care of Corinne? But she did not have time to answer her own questions, for Randolf had finished shouting at the men and had come over to her. He was blazing with rage.

'What in the name of hell are you and your sister doing here, Diana Skelton? Didn't you know that it would be a dangerous place? Why couldn't you stop Corinne running to Zach Netheroyd like that? My militia had

162

orders to fire into the ground to anyone who moved. And they shot not a cropper, but a silly girl, who, from what I heard, seems to be your Gilbert's love. Stay in the counting-house until I come. I have to speak to the men.'

The crowd of men, by this time, were uneasy. They had expected the militia, but they had not expected them to shoot at the slightest provocation. And the old master's daughter shot? Things were not going according to plan. Zach should never have run forward on his own, they were muttering amongst themselves.

They watched soberly as the small party of Mr Dyke carrying Miss Corinne followed by Miss Skelton and Zach, moved into the counting-house. They themselves were ready to disperse, but they were stopped by the sound of the master's voice and they watched in amazement as Samuel Topping came out of the counting-house carrying a chair which he set down in front of them.

Then Randolf climbed up on the chair and faced them, he seemed a figure towering above them, the Redcoats were behind him.

'My men,' Randolf said loudly and clearly, 'and I call you that sincerely. Almost every one of you here tonight works in my mill or have worked in my mill in the past. You were angry and I can understand that; you were angry that I had taken your work from you and that your families were suffering. I can understand that, too. But I will tell you this. In the weeks since I laid you off, I have been desperately seeking work for you.'

He paused as though he was looking at each one in that crowd. 'I am speaking now to my croppers, those of you who were here to smash the very frames which will in time give you more work . . . '

'What kind o' work then?' someone shouted.

'It won't be cropping for the machines do that now, but I am

164

determined to have work for you all. Until that time comes, will you please listen to me and to what I have been trying to do on your behalf. Now, you all know the land between the mill and Mill House; there are two large fields.'

'What good is that to the likes of us,' came another voice, loud and surly.

'Just listen, please. I am not a rich man as you might suppose, all my money went in buying Keld Mill and now I have spent almost my very last penny buying those fields. Listen, please. What I propose is this. The fields are to be divided into strips and each man of you who has lost his work in the mill will be given a strip for himself. There will be no rent to be paid.

'On that strip, you can grow what you like. Enough vegetables to feed your family, if you like; or enough to take to Huddersfield market to sell. Either way, it will help you through a lean time and I am going to make a promise that until the time you have some produce from your strip of land, I will pay each man a small allowance to feed his family. That will be from my own pocket.'

A murmur went through the crowd as he stopped speaking, and Randolf paused to let the idea sink in. then he added clearly. 'What is more, when the mill is working to the full again and you have your employment back, you can keep the strip as a recompense for being out of work all that time. Can I be fairer than that?'

There was a buzz amongst the men; they had listened silently and carefully and now, all seemed to be talking at once.

Randolf continued as soon as they became quiet again. 'One last word . . . We will have no more grumbling, or anger or plotting against me and I will not seek punishment for your work this night — not even for you, Zachariah Netheroyd, for I understand how you feel. Now go home peacefully and tell your wives what I have told you; you can be proud of living in Holmby and being within sight of the mill. There is no need for violence and there will be no violence. Goodnight, brothers.'

Amongst the crowd, Diana thought there were murmurings of assent and a few 'Ays' could be heard; they drifted slowly away convinced by a master of rhetoric and by sound commonsense that there were better things to come. Zach was almost the last to leave and he took Small Zach with him.

Randolf had stepped down from his chair and caught sight of Diana; he walked towards her with a rueful grin. 'I am not in the least pleased with you, Diana, but I have done all I can for my workers, all we have suffered is a few broken windows and a shot to the leg of your silly little sister. How is she? I will speak to you later about your reasons for being here at a very dangerous time.'

Inside the counting-house, they found Corinne drowsy from the laudanum Mr Pennycross had given her; he had removed the ball from her leg and pronounced that the wound had not been deep and would soon heal.

He had bandaged her leg and she lay there, still in her cloak and with Gilbert holding her hand.

She managed a smile when she saw Randolf. 'I am sorry, Randolf, I should not have run after Small Zach and Gilbert is very cross with me.'

'So Gilbert might be,' Randolf observed, looking down at her. 'But it did show the men that the Redcoats were ready to fire at the slightest movement. I am not in the least pleased with you and Diana being there at all and I have no wish to hold you up as a heroine, but the fact remains that the rebels were silenced when you were shot. It gave me the opportunity of speaking to them. They are dispersing now, I am pleased to say.' He turned to Diana. 'Now we have to think of how to get your sister back to Keld Head House.'

Gilbert spoke then and his reply came quickly. 'I think the best plan would be for me to ride back to Cannock Hall and then to bring my carriage for Corinne. I will take her there and my mother will look after her.'

He bent towards Corinne and squeezed her hand. 'Did you hear that, my dear? Stay just where you are while I fetch the carriage, then I will carry you out to it. You will not mind staying at Cannock Hall? We will be very pleased to have you until you are better.'

'You are very kind to me, Gilbert, I will do just as you say and I will try not to complain if my leg hurts. I am sorry if I did the wrong thing but I could only think of Small Zach. Where is he?'

Diana, who had been watching this scene with amusement now that she could see that Corinne was recovering, looked around her, but could see neither Zach or the boy.

'I think his father must have taken him home,' she said and glanced down at her sister who looked as pretty as ever. 'Gilbert has been very kind to you,' she remarked drily.

'Oh, Diana, he is so good; and to offer to have me at Cannock Hall. You don't mind, are you sure?'

'No, of course I don't mind, I will ride over in the morning and bring you some dresses and things . . . goodness gracious, it must be nearly morning now.'

Sam Topping who had stood silently by while all this was going on, looked at the clock on the counting-house wall. 'It's coming up to midnight, miss.' He looked at her as though something had occurred to him. 'But, Miss Diana, how are you going to go back home? You can't walk on your own at this time of night. I had better come along of you.'

'I know the lane well, thank you, Sam. I will be all right.'

A voice was heard from the doorway. 'You will not go on your own,' Randolf Staines said sternly. 'I will fetch the trap and I will take you home. There are many things I wish to say to you.'

'I have no doubt of that,' came the swift retort from Diana. 'I can quite easily walk and I will set off as soon as Gilbert has taken Corinne.'

'You will do no such thing. You will go in my trap even if I have to carry you as Gilbert intends to carry Corinne.'

'I am rather large to be carried, sir,' she said, with a pretence at sweetness.

'Be quiet, you will do as I say and if we are to have words, it will not be in front of everyone else. Sit down with Corinne and watch out for the Dyke carriage.'

'Yes, Randolf,' she replied with seeming meekness.

Gilbert was not long in returning to the mill and he went straight into the counting-house to find Diana sitting with Corinne and no sign of Randolf.

Diana had said very little to her sister during Gilbert's short absence; Corinne was still sleepy and Diana looked up as Gilbert approached and she put a finger to her lips.

'She is very drowsy, Gilbert.'

He nodded. 'Yes, I expect she is. It is the laudanum, but it was wise of Mr Pennycross to give it for she won't feel the pain in her leg quite so much. Poor little dear.'

'Poor little nothing, Gilbert, it was extremely foolish of her to dash forward like that.'

Gilbert looked shocked. 'But Corinne is injured, Diana, do you feel no sympathy for her?'

'Very little, though I notice that you are more than sympathetic.'

'Of course I am,' he replied shortly. 'I am very fond of little Corinne, I always have been.'

'I fancy it is more than a fondness,' said Diana. 'But now is not the time to talk of it. I will help you lift her into the carriage.'

She saw them being driven off and wondered what to do next. There was no sign of Randolf and she guessed that he was making sure that all was in order in the mill before fetching the trap. The Redcoats were still standing in a line by the door.

Sam Topping came from the direction of the mill and looked concerned when he saw her. 'Are you waiting for master, Miss Diana?'

'I cannot see him anywhere, Sam, so I will walk on . . . '

'Miss Diana,' Sam exclaimed in horror. 'You can't be walking up that lane by yourself and in the dark, too.'

'I know every hole in the road, Sam, I won't come to any harm. Please tell Mr Staines when he appears.'

'He'll be angry, Miss Diana, you can be sure of it. Settled them men right and proper, he did, but I can't vouch for his temper if I let you go on your own.'

'Sam, you are needed here and he will be even more angry if you leave the counting-house. Do not be in a worry about me. I bid you goodnight.'

Diana walked away without another word and Sam, knowing that it would cost him his place if he left the mill, watched her walk out of the gates. He had grave misgivings. 'Always was headstrong, Miss Diana,' he muttered to himself. 'Would do nicely for master if she weren't to wed Mr Dyke.'

Diana was soon out of the village and while she had buildings about her, she had felt confident; but once on her own in the lane up the hill, she began to feel uneasy. The ground was rough, and the pot-holes which she knew well by daylight, seemed like traps waiting for her faltering steps.

When she heard the sound of a horse, and wheels bumping furiously over those same pot-holes, she did not have to wait for Randolf's furious shout to know that he had come after her.

She stepped to one side as he pulled level with her and quickly jumped down beside her.

'If you are not the most infuriating girl I ever had the misfortune to meet. Why could you have not waited a moment? I had to go up to the house to fetch the trap. You might have known. And how could you manage to walk on this infernal lane on such a dark night?' he asked with explosive anger.

'I couldn't,' she replied sweetly. 'I was beginning to trip in every hole, I was quite glad to hear the trap.'

'Trollop,' he said rudely. 'Get into the trap for heaven's sake.'

Diana climbed up on to the trap beside Randolf and he did not attempt to help her. He is in a surly mood, she told herself, and said nothing.

Indeed, not a word was said between them all the way up to the house; Diana felt obstinate and not repentant. They stopped at the front door and Randolf spoke at last; they were not the words Diana was expecting to hear.

'Well, Miss Skelton, are you going to ask me in?'

She was jerked into astonishment. 'Ask you in, Randolf, when it must be nearly one o'clock in the morning and not a soul in the house except for the servants? My father is away in Leeds. What are you thinking of?'

He turned to look at her. 'My first

thought, my dear Diana . . . '

'I am not your dear anything.'

'Miss Skelton, then. My first thought is that I would like a large glass of brandy. My second thought is that I need to be very angry with you, and I feel that sitting outside on a trap in the middle of the night, is not the right place. Let me help you down.'

He had jumped down from the trap and stood at her side, holding out a hand.

Diana was at a loss. She needed to explain her actions to him and did agree that the words would be more easily said if she and Randolf were inside the house. It was against the properties, but cook and the servants were all indoors. Suddenly, she was beyond caring about the conversations. If she and the mill owner were to have words then they would be more easily said in the privacy of her own drawing-room.

In the entrance-hall, they were greeted by a worried-looking Ellen.

'Miss Diana — oh, and Mr Staines — I were that bothered you being so long and where is Miss Corinne then?'

Diana's reply was unnecessarily terse. 'Miss Corinne is staying at Cannock Hall. Please bring some brandy for Mr Staines, and I will have some chocolate.'

'Yes, miss, and I kept the fire going just in case.'

Diana softened a little. 'Thank you, Ellen, that was thoughtful of you.'

In the drawing-room, Ellen brought their drinks and Diana was silent. She was sitting by the fire, glad of its warmth. Randolf stood with his back to it, his brandy glass in his hand.

One of us got to speak first, she was thinking, the silence was awkward.

When Randolf at last spoke, his words came slowly and courteously. 'I will try not to lose my temper, Diana, but I wish to hear why you should have been in the mill yard at the same time as the men forced the gates. Could you not sense danger? And damn it all, woman, you had Corinne and the boy with you, as well.'

Diana stood up and faced him; she could see steely anger in his eyes. 'How dare you speak to me like that and before you have heard a word of explanation.'

'You were there and that is all there is to it and why in the name of God almighty did you have Corinne? Give me a reason for that. Not only that, you did not keep a hold on her. As soon as there was trouble, she rushes into the middle of it and was shot. It was your doing, Miss Diana Skelton, and I demand an explanation for your deucedly stupid actions at such a time . . .'

He was not allowed to finish. Diana, full of an ungovernable rage struck at him; she put her full force behind the blow. His head jerked back and he uttered two words.

'You hellcat.' And seizing her by the waist, he pulled her up against him.

'No . . . ' she cried out.

'Yes,' came the reply as his lips were

on hers in a kiss which almost hurt her; but just as she began struggling, his arms slackened and the kiss became passionate. When it came to an end, they stared at each other. Diana overwhelmed by her feelings, Randolf penitent and saying so.

'Diana, my dearest girl, what can I say? I apologise. Did you not realise that I feared for you when I saw you there at the mill?'

Diana sat down in the chair and she did not know if the tears streaming down her cheeks were of love or repentance. 'Randolf, I am sorry that it happened like that. I had come to warn you that Annie had sent a message by Small Zach that the men were attacking the mill tonight. Corinne would not let me come on my own.'

'I begin to understand,' he said.

'Of course, it turned out I was too late and you know what happened then; and Gilbert with a musket, too, I couldn't believe it.'

'He has been very helpful, your Gilbert.'

She looked at him and gave a grin. 'I am not sure if he is my Gilbert any more.'

'You mean Corinne?'

'Yes, I think he has loved her all this time and I wish them joy.'

He bent down and kissed her cheek. 'So, my dearest girl, we have your Gilbert at Corinne's side and calling her his love. How very encouraging. Do you realise that it leaves me free to ask you to marry me, and for the third time, I believe.'

'We would fight,' she said robustly, but her heart was pounding.

'No matter,' he replied and with a happy smile. 'We would also love. Do you love me, Diana, just as I love you?'

She gazed at him with a sudden feeling of great happiness. 'You love me, Randolf?'

'From the moment I first entered this very room,' he said softly. 'I was determined to have you as my wife.'

'But . . . ' she started to say.

'No buts, I am going to kiss you again.'

This time, the kiss was long and tender and Diana knew she was where she wanted to be.

'Now tell me, Diana.'

'I do love you, Randolf,' she whispered. 'I love you very much.'

THE END

We do hope that you have enjoyed reading this large print book.

Did you know that all of our titles are available for purchase?

We publish a wide range of high quality large print books including:
Romances, Mysteries, Classics
General Fiction
Non Fiction and Westerns

Special interest titles available in large print are:
The Little Oxford Dictionary
Music Book, Song Book
Hymn Book, Service Book

Also available from us courtesy of Oxford University Press:
Young Readers' Dictionary
(large print edition)
Young Readers' Thesaurus
(large print edition)

For further information or a free brochure, please contact us at:
Ulverscroft Large Print Books Ltd.,
The Green, Bradgate Road, Anstey,
Leicester, LE7 7FU, England.
Tel: (00 44) **0116 236 4325**
Fax: (00 44) **0116 234 0205**

TOO CLOSE FOR COMFORT

Chrissie Loveday

Emily has shut herself away to work in the family's old holiday cottage in remotest West Cornwall. Her two Jack Russells are all the company she needs . . . until the night she rescues a stranger injured in a raging storm. Cut off by bad weather, and with no telephone, they have to sit it out. Emily begins to warm to Adam. But who is he — and why does he want to stay with her once the storm has passed?

CHRISTMAS CHARADE

Kay Gregory

When Nina Petrov meets charismatic businessman Fenton Hardwick on a transcontinental train to Chicago, she sees him as the solution to her recurring Christmas problem. Every year her matchmaking father produces a different hopelessly unsuitable man for her to marry. Nina decides she needs a temporary fiancé to get him off her case, and Fen seems the perfect candidate for the job — until she makes the mistake of trying to pay him for his help . . .

A LETTER TO MY LOVE

Toni Anders

Devastated when Marcus married someone else, Sorrel resolved to devote her life to her toyshop and her invalid cousin, Alyse. However, when she meets Carl, the Bavarian woodcarver, it provides a romantic distraction — but Marcus's growing friendship with Alyse unsettles Sorrel. She is torn between her still-present love for Marcus, and her cousin's happiness. When Marcus's spiteful sister, Pamela, decides to repossess the toyshop for a wine bar, Sorrel decides to fight them both.

DOCTOR, DOCTOR

Chrissie Loveday

The arrival of a new doctor in a small Cornish hospital causes a stir, especially among the female members of staff. Lauren has worked hard to build her career, along with a protective shell to keep her emotions intact. She won't risk being hurt again, but Tom has other ideas . . . As they share the highs and lows of hospital life, they develop a mutual respect for each other's professional skills — but can there ever be more to their relationship?